Kathy,

Congrats on the win!
Enjoy the adventure!

Jill Edick
8/1/10

P.S. Pineapple wine is real
& delicious!

♡ Maui
Speech

Truly

JILL EDICK

authorHOUSE

AuthorHouse™
1663 Liberty Drive
Bloomington, IN 47403
www.authorhouse.com
Phone: 1 (800) 839-8640

© 2016 Jill Edick. All rights reserved.

No part of this book may be reproduced, stored in a retrieval system, or transmitted by any means without the written permission of the author.

Published by AuthorHouse 04/19/2016

ISBN: 978-1-5246-0456-1 (sc)
ISBN: 978-1-5246-0455-4 (e)

Print information available on the last page.

Any people depicted in stock imagery provided by Thinkstock are models, and such images are being used for illustrative purposes only.
Certain stock imagery © Thinkstock.

This book is printed on acid-free paper.

Because of the dynamic nature of the Internet, any web addresses or links contained in this book may have changed since publication and may no longer be valid. The views expressed in this work are solely those of the author and do not necessarily reflect the views of the publisher, and the publisher hereby disclaims any responsibility for them.

Dedication

To my beautiful daughter who encouraged me to write,

My husband who put up with me writing,

And my Best Friend Jodi my personal "Cera".

Thank you for your love and support, not to mention a few bottles of Pineapple Wine!

Prologue

As I stand behind her, watching her stare at the sky, I am afraid. Have I lost her?

As I sit alone on the cool park bench, I can' t help but wonder what is happening on the other side of the world. As our night sky darkens and the stars start to make their appearance, I wonder as I look up, can the people across the world see the same stars as I? And I'm thinking where is my heart right now? Is he thinking of me? What happened to my life? Will I ever feel whole again?

A Time for Everything

There is a time for everything, and a season
for every activity under the heavens:

A time to be born and a time to die, a time to plant and a time to uproot, a time to kill and a time to heal, a time to tear down and a time to build, a time to weep and a time to laugh, a time to mourn and a time to dance, a time to scatter stones and a time to gather them, a time to embrace and a time to refrain, a time to search and a time to give up, a time to keep and a time to throw away, a time to tear and a time to mend, a time to be silent and a time to speak, a time to love and a time to hate, a time for war and a time for peace.

Ecclesiastes 3:1-8

Part 1

Chapter 1

"Darlena! I didn't know you were in today! I thought you had off to prepare for your fabulous party this weekend!"

"Hi Maggie. I was going to take off, but really I already have the party under control and the kids still have school for a couple more days, do I decided to come in and stay ahead of the notes!"

I'm Darlena. I prefer to be called Lena, but for some reason, only my best friend can manage to remember that. My husband and mother call me Dar. I really hate it, but I can't seem to break them of it either. I work part time at a small doctor's office in Flourtown Pennsylvania. My husband is a stock broker and works on wall street. He commutes to New York and stays for the weekdays at a small apartment there. Every year for Memorial day, I host a large garden party for our friends, neighbors, coworkers and family. It's quite an event usually and in the past I have spent weeks getting ready for it.

I haven't felt it this year though. I'm not sure why. Maybe it's because my husband has been gone, often for more than a week, for work. It makes me upset, but when we argue, he makes a good point. We live in a beautiful neighborhood with great schools for our girls. I don't have to work; I do though to have something to do during the day while the girls are at school. He makes great money. But I miss him. And lately it seems he is gone longer and longer and home less and less.

We have three beautiful girls. They are all in school now and heavy into activities and friends. They have sports or clubs in the afternoons, games or events on the weekends. And always something important to do with a friend or fifty! They don't miss their dad as much as they used to. One would think I wouldn't either since I'm always so busy with working part time and being a fulltime driver for the girls the rest of the time.

Jill Edick

I get lonely though. I miss Geoffrey. We met in college. I was a freshman and he a junior. We dated until he graduated. He was preparing to start school for a masters when we discovered I was pregnant with our first daughter Melinda. We got a small apartment together and got married quietly at the courthouse. I dropped out of school to be a full time mom while he continued to work on his degree. We lived on student loans and help from our families. We struggled a lot until he completed his degree and stared working full time. After he received his masters and started working, we became pregnant with our twins Melissa and Melanie. We struggled with the bills because I wasn't working, but decided that the cost of child care far outweighed the benefits of a second income. So he started looking for jobs outside of State College where we went to school. He found an entry level position with the brokerage firm he currently works for. But it required a move. I didn't want to move to New York, not that we could have afforded that anyway. So we moved to Philly where he could commute easier into the city. It was hard at first because we now had two rents to pay plus all of the loans and 3 children. But he rapidly climbed the ladder and soon bills were paid and we bought a house and things were looking up. But I was starting to feel the anxiety even then of seeing him only on weekends and raising our girls alone. But he was so attentive on the weekends and the girls loved seeing him and we would shop and eat out and have fun. So I would keep quiet on Sunday night when he left for New York. But my heart broke a little each time.

We bought our house Flourtown when Melinda turned 6. We wanted a nice neighborhood to raise them with good schools. Our house was way out of our budget, but Geoffrey was confident, we could make it happen. So we took the plunge. And he started coming home only three weekends a month.

I decided I needed some adult companionship during the week. As much as I loved the girls, they were not the same as adults. My best friend and I talked weekly and saw each other as often as she was around. She travels for her job. She works for some scientific company that studies dirt from around the world. I call her the dirt whisperer. I actually have no idea what she does, but she is gone a lot and has seen some of the most amazing places in the world. I tell her all the time how jealous I am. She reminds me, I have a home and family and how jealous she is. We are best friends though. I know if I ever needed her, she would be by my side in a heartbeat. But I still needed some more friends. So the annual Memorial Day party started.

I made friends with many of the neighbors and moms of my daughters friends. It was great. My husband would take a week off to help me and we put on an amazing spread.

After the twins started school, I decided to take a part time job typing transcription for a local doctor. It worked great with my girl's schedule and I met more friends, and my annual party grew.

Now my oldest is fourteen and the twins are twelve and my husband will be flying in Saturday morning for the party and leaving again that night after the party. I have been doing it so long, I don't need to plan anymore, I just call the vendors I have used for years and order what I want and give them the credit card. Everyone still loves the party and raves about it. I have gotten bored with it, and my husband doesn't care any longer, he barely even shows up. But this year Cera my best friend will be in town and will be there. So for that I am still excited.

I finished with the last dictation I had from the doctor and told the office manager I was leaving. The whole office would be at the party. So none minded that I was leaving early or took tomorrow off.

Before I could pick up the girls from school though, I promised Cera I would pick her up from the airport. I was so excited, it was like being a school girl and going to my first dance. She will be staying with me for a week before she has to leave to go on her next fabulous trip. She told me she had the most fabulous gift for me when she got here. I hate surprises and she knows this, which is why she does these things. It's pure evil, but her gifts are super fabulous. She never forgets a birthday, holiday's or special occasion and amazing things always show up in the mail from all over the world. The girls call her Auntie Cece. They love her at least as much as I do. Lindy (what my oldest prefers to be called) even loves her so much she volunteered to "be seen with the brat twins" and wait for them after school and walk home with them if I couldn't get there in time to pick them up. No doubt that meant walking ahead of them by at least a block, but the twins are old enough to make it on their own, I just insist on "safety in numbers". The girls say I'm paranoid and weird. I'm ok with that.

I pulled up to the airport pickup spot and Cera was waiting. She jumped in the car and we hugged quickly so we didn't get yelled at by security. It was so great to have her here with me. We talked and laughed all the way to the house. We pulled up into the drive way and started to walk into the house.

"Auntie CECE!!" Three voices and streaks of brown hair blew past me and knocked Cera out the front door and onto the lawn in a heap of laughter.

"Girls! Get off Cera! Let her breathe! She just got here and you literally ran her out the door!"

All four came back into the house laughing and hugging.

"Lena, just relax, your just mad because the girls will get their presents first and you have to wait! HA HA HA HA HA HA!"

"Your evil woman!"

I left the girls to grill Cera about her latest adventures and talk her out of presents. I went to prepare a real home cooked dinner for Cera. I always tried to cook for her as she ate out everywhere she traveled. She had some stories about food she had ate.

After several hours of laughter and fun. I sent the girls to bed reminding them that their last day of school was tomorrow. After much groaning and whining, they finally went to their rooms. I doubt to bed, but at least Cera and I were about to get some time alone.

"So dear Lena, lets crack open some Cab and I'll give you're your present."

"You have already given me presents. What more could you have?"

"Well let's open the wine and then take a look!"

Truly

I left to get a bottle of wine while Cera grabbed her bag and settled into a comfy chair in the living room.

I joined her a minute later with the wine.

I was sitting opposite her and she tossed an envelope in my lap. I opened it and was looking at a plane ticket.

"What's this?"

"Well my dear that is called a plane ticket."

"I'm aware it's a plane ticket, silly, but I can't go anywhere."

"First, why not? Will the world stop if you're not here? Second, why the hell not? And Finally, why the fricking hell not? Are you afraid hubby dearest won't let you? Screw that!"

Cera never minced words, I both loved and hated that. She also does not care for my husband. She says he is a pompous arrogant ass. And yes, that is true, but he is kind and wonderful and takes care of the girls and I. She just doesn't see that part of him.

"Well, to answer your so eloquently asked questions, first, who would take care of the kids, I see only one ticket, and I can't imagine going on a family trip without Geoff anyway. Second, because. Finally, If I wanted to go, I'm sure Geoff would let me, not that I have to ask permission. But, there is the small problem of the girls. He works, in another state, remember? It just isn't possible for me to up and leave."

"You haven't even looked at the ticket to see where we are going. The girls are old enough to stay with friends or family. And really, your husband can't take some time off to take care of his own kids? Seriously! I love the girls too! Couldn't love them more if they were mine, but you are an individual, who has adult needs and wants too! Your husband got to complete his wants and finish school and found an amazing job with no household responsibility but send home a pay check. You are a mom. And that's a HUGE job. Toughest there is, with no pay! But you are also a human, and somewhere along the way that got lost. You CAN be a mom and still get to have fun and take care of you! Dammit Lena!"

Cera slammed back the glass of wine in her hand and refilled it and took another long deep drink.

She grabbed the ticket from me, opened it up and held it in front of me. I looked at it. It said Bangkok. Thailand. OH MY GOD! She got me a ticket to Thailand. She remembered. In middle school geography class, I did my presentation on Thailand and since had always dreamed of going. Geoffrey said he had no desire to see the orient, too dirty and nasty eating habits. The only trips he would consider involved a cruise ship or island beach in the Bahamas. Not that we had gone on more than two family trips, and both of them he spent most of his time on his phone or computer working. He sent me and the kids to Disney World once. He was supposed to join us on the trip, but couldn't get away from work. I always felt like he never intended to go to Disney with us, but he denied it when I once asked.

"Thailand? Cera! Oh my goodness, THAILAND! Hold it, you said we, are you going too?"

"Of course! I sadly get to have only one week of this trip as pleasure before I have to return to work, however, you will get the full three weeks to explore, site see, rest relax, build sand castles at the beach resort, whatever you want! I know you hate having someone work on vacation, but when I get back to the hotel each night, my shit gets turned off, promise right now! And our first week it doesn't go on. Nothing but CeraLena time! So, are you ready to do this?!"

CeraLena time, Thailand, two of the most wonderful thoughts I could think. I loved the girls, and three weeks, was so long. But how could I possibly say no? How could I go? How could I not?

I looked up at Cera with glassy eyes, "Of course I'm going. But you have to help figure out how!"

She smiled, refilled both our glasses! "I'll drink to that!" we tapped glasses and I knew, not how, but I knew I was about to live a dream!

In another state:

"Seriously! I thought you weren't going! Do you have to leave now? I promise I can entertain you better."

She wiggles her bare ass in the air.

"Believe me, I know you can." He slaps her ass hard leaving a mark. "I'll be back for that soon. Keep it warmed up for me."

"Warm it up yourself, NOW!"

Chapter 2

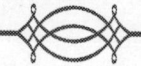

I drove the girls to their last day of school the next morning. Cera drank a bit too much the night before and had yet to make an appearance. But I could not miss the last day. That always involved as much picture taking as the first for me, much to the girl's disgust. But it was Lindy's last day in middle school, next year she was going to high school! And the twins were finishing their first year of middle school with honors at the top of their class! The least they could do is fake a few smiles for last day pictures!

To my surprise, Cera was up and on the phone with a notebook spread out in front of her gabbing and writing like there was no tomorrow. She gave me a wave and I went to get a cup of coffee.

Cera ended her call and tossed her phone on the notepad and grabbed my coffee from me. She winked and took a drink.

"Well my dear, I have the kids all squared away, and the dogs too. I found a very reasonable house service that will take care of mail, papers and checking on things for you, they came highly recommended. The only thing left is for you to have the party of the year, and deal with your asshole…I mean husband!"

"Wow, well so many questions come to mind, where to start?" I took my coffee cup back from Cera and refilled it. "So, where, what, who and how on earth did you get that done in the fifteen minutes I was gone? And can you please tell me why you hate my husband so much? I never could figure that out."

"Ha ha my dear! You forget how amazing I am! The girls are off for a three-week adventure to Colorado! They will be staying with my family in Boulder. My sister was so excited that she already started planning camping and hiking and shopping and on and on. You know how she is.

Truly

The girls are going to have a blast! The dogs are going to a luxury doggie hotel and spa. They have their own room with an outdoor run. They get walks daily which I dare say is more than they get with you, oh and daily massage treatments. And there is a pool. I don't know why dogs need a pool or massages, but there you have it. They are taken care of. Your neighbor gave me the name of the house watching company. Great people, good prices, even better if your louse actually comes home on weekends and takes care of his own shit. I got it all done because I am truly gifted and an awesome friend."

"In other words, you had most of this figured out before you even showed up."

"Correctomundo!"

"Pretty confident aren't you? You still didn't answer why you hate Geoffrey so much."

"Ah, the husband. I don't hate him; I just think you could do so much better. I know he has a great paycheck, but isn't there more to marriage? I just think there should be."

"There is, you just don't see it. I know he's gone a lot, but love must count for something, and he does love us."

"Of course sweetie, I'm sure he does. I love you too, my best friend and I worry, that's part of my job. Just like I know I can count on good food when I come to visit and I know I won't have to eat out! I promise, I will lighten up on Geoffrey, ok?"

"Okay. I don't know that I believe you completely, you always have reasons for your feelings, but I will let it rest. Thank you. Now, I have a long list of chores for this party tomorrow! Why don't you get ready and help me tackle this day!"

The kids got out of school at noon, so we picked them up and came home with loads of decorations. The canopy, chairs and tables were there being set up and we all dove in for decorating.

We had fairy lights up and flowers and streamers everywhere. Potted plants had been delivered and set up around the canopy, and fresh flower centerpieces on every table. The place looked spectacular. There were a few more things to be delivered in the morning. But all in all this was the fastest and most beautiful job that I had ever done. Having Cera and the girls help was immeasurable.

Just for Cera, I had all the ingredients for homemade pizza including my famous sauce, freshly grated cheese and dough I had prepared yesterday just for this. Of course a few more bottles of Cab had shown up and we had the best night cooking and playing games with the girls until we all fell asleep in the living room.

When I woke in the morning, the twins and one dog were curled up with Cera on the couch, and Lindy and the smaller dog was with me in my oversized chair. I sat taking in this site and smiling. It was such a fun scene. What fabulous memories we made last night. I hoped Geoff would be ok with the trip and the girls with their own little trip.

The front door flew with a whoosh of air and hit the wall with a bang and the whole of the peace was shattered. Lissa and Lanie jumped and screamed and the dogs were across the room barking before I was even on my feet. Cera, Lindy and I were up and moving towards the door when the dogs stopped barking and we heard, "Shut up mutts, you're going to wake the whole damn house!"

Geoffrey was home.

"Geoff! Why didn't you call, I would have picked you up, I wasn't expecting you so soon!"

I ran to my husband to give him a hug and kiss. It had been over two weeks since he had been home last. The girls were all up and composed and moving towards Geoff as well.

"What is going on out here? Why are you all in the living room? Cera, what are you doing here? Aren't you supposed to be in Egypt or someplace playing in the mud?"

"Geoff, be nice, you know Cera is here for the party! How did you get home?"

The girls gave their dad hugs but there was certainly none of the enthusiasm that I had seen when Cera arrived. I guess I had noticed the lack of enthusiasm before, but I just attributed it to the girls getting older and certainly more hormonal. But something in the reaction struck me this morning. And Geoff seemed so angry. Had I forgotten something? I started going through my mental list to figure out what I could have done.

"I'm sorry my ladies! I'm really tired today. I knew I wasn't going to be able to make my regular shuttle home, so I tried alternative transport. Go outside and take a look girls!" With that the old Geoff seemed to return, there was a genuine smile on his face. "I hope you like it beautiful, it's for you. I had to drive it home last night for you. Sorry if I'm grumpy, I need a couple hours of shut eye, a shower and some of your sweet cooking!" He planted an amazingly passionate kiss on me, one the likes of which I hadn't felt in a long time. "Come on, let's go outside!"

I looked at Cera and smiled. She smiled back. "I think I will let the family have this moment, I'm going to go hit the shower, I think more deliveries will be arriving soon. Good to see you Geoffrey." She didn't say that last part with much feeling as she turned and walked away.

Geoff grabbed my hand and led me outside. In the driveway was a beautiful new Jaguar. It was dark green and sleek. A stunning car. Certainly fancier then the SUV I currently drove, but also extremely impractical, which was why I had the SUV.

"Wow Geoff, it's beautiful. Just stunning. I'm not sure how I will fit the girls and all their stuff in it, but I know we will have fun cruising the neighborhood in it! Thank you!"

"Your welcome, and I don't think this is a kid car. It's for you to drive to go out with friends or for us to use. I never want to see a dog hair in here Dar. This is a nice car. Not like that beast you drive for kid and dog stuff.'"

Jill Edick

"Kid and dog stuff? I believe the words your looking for are family functions? I like the car, why are you so defensive?"

"I'm not defensive, but I can't ever seem to get you anything you love any more. I'm trying here and all you can think about is how un-family friendly this is. Can't you just like it? Cripes! I'm going to go rest. Keys in the car. Do whatever with it."

He stormed away leaving me and the girls in his wake wondering what just happened?

Lindy walked up and held my hand. "It's ok mom, he's just tired. He will be better later. Let's just go inside and get ready for the deliveries Auntie CECE mentioned. We have a party to get ready for."

"Yeah mommy" both twins chimed in. Then I was wrapped in 3 sets of arms for a mommy sandwich hug.

We went into the house and started getting ready for the day ahead. Cera was right, vendors would be showing up soon and there was lots to do.

When I came in the house Cera met me in the living room where she was picking up stuff from the night before. "So, a new car huh? That's nice. Did you want a jag? I always though you more of a Porsche girl." We both started laughing. Truth be told, I loved my SUV. Any sports car was more Geoff's style than mine. But now I had a jag and had to deal with it.

"I don't care about cars, you know that. What bothers me though is how angry Geoff got. He knows me enough that he should have known a car wouldn't excite me. I tried to be excited, I really did. I just don't care about cars. I'm such a bad wife."

"You are not a bad wife Lena. You have a right to like or not like anything. Yes, he got you a car, but wouldn't it have been nicer if he came home and took you shopping? Don't take the blame for his anger. Shame on him for making you feel bad."

Truly

"Well, maybe I should go talk to him. This is a conversation I should have with him. I'm sure we can talk it out and both be happy. Plus, I need to talk to him about the trip. That is soon, and he leaves after the party tonight, so maybe I better go and talk to him."

"Ok. Good luck Lena. I'm going to get the girls and get outside to wait for more vendors. I will take care of that for now, come on out when you're ready."

I went upstairs and heard Geoff in our room talking to someone. When I went in I saw he was on his phone, definitely not resting. I closed the door and sat on the edge of our bed to wait for him to end his call.

"I have to go, we will talk more later... NO, I will call you back. You know I'm busy today... Goodbye."

He tossed his phone on the bed and started to walk into the bathroom.

"Geoff, can we talk please?"

"About what Dar? I need a shower."

"Well I want to talk about the car but also about something else."

"There is nothing to talk about the car. I like it, I bought it as a gift for you. If you don't like it, go buy your own and I'll keep it. End of discussion. What else?"

"Why are you so angry? I don't know what I did. I was just surprised about the car. I like it very much. It will be a nice car for us. Please quit being so angry."

"You said there was something else, what is it? I really need to rest awhile and I have an early flight back tonight."

"An early flight? What about the party? Aren't you staying until the end? Surely you can at least stay until it's over. Your never here much anymore. Can you really not stay and go back tomorrow?"

Jill Edick

"You know I can't. Someone has to pay the bills. You like this lifestyle, it requires payment. I have to work to keep this up for you. Then I buy you a nice gift and you bash it. Now I have paid for a waste. I have to go back to work to pay for that and to get you what you really want. This isn't easy for me either. You're here spending money on parties while I work there and when I'm home for a day I get nothing but bitched at. What do you want from me Dar? Huh? What?"

"I want you to be home like you used to. I don't need fancy stuff. And if the party is too much, I won't do it again. We can cut back. The girls and I are happy, but we don't need things to keep it that way. We need you! We miss you! I'm sorry you think you need to work so hard and be gone so much to give us things. You don't! Please. Let's go back to the way we were. Let's remember what we used to love about each other and start enjoying each other more and things less! Please Geoff."

We stared silently at each other. This wasn't the first argument like this we had had. Unfortunately. But it never seemed to change. We had this lifestyle that we couldn't seem to get away from, or maybe deep down we didn't want to. I wasn't sure. I just know I missed my relationship with Geoff.

"I'm sorry Dar. I know you don't want 'things'. I like our lives now though. I don't want to go back to being broke and borrowing money from our parents for groceries. I like my job. I like my little space in New York. I don't know how we compromise on that. I want to see you more too, but it just isn't possible with our lives right now. But I'm doing this for us, for our future, for early retirement and the ability to enjoy that retirement comfortably and debt free. Let's not fight. I know how much you enjoy this party and you work so hard. I will make some calls and see if I can't stay until morning ok?"

"I'm sorry to Geoff. I love you! Please, see if you can stay tonight. I miss you so much!"

I walked over to him and put my arms around him for a hug, that wasn't reciprocated.

"You said you had something else Dar?"

"Yes, I do. Cera got me a gift as well. She bought me a ticket to go with her on her next work trip. She is going to Thailand. It would cost us nothing, I will be staying with her and she's paying for everything. Would you mind if I went? Thailand has always been a dream for me."

"A trip? She shows up with a 'work trip' to some nasty eastern place and your excited, I arrive home with a new Jaguar and you get pissy? Are you serious Dar? Are you fucking serious?"

It was like I had just been slapped. I was shocked. We had argued before, but he had never cursed at me like this before.

"I, I'm sorry. I didn't think you would be angry about it. There is no expense to us, and your home so little anyway, but I don't have to go. I'll just go tell Cera, hopefully she bought insurance on the ticket."

I turned and ran out of the room as the tears started to fall. I felt like my dreams were washing away with each tear that fell. And not just my dream to go to Thailand, but my marriage, my happy life. Everything.

I wasn't paying attention and ran right into Cera.

"I heard everything, no words necessary. Come, you need to sit and calm down before the girls see you."

She took me into her room and I sat in a chair and cried for about 15 minutes. When I finally stopped, she took me into the bathroom to wash my face and clean up.

"I will talk to Geoff. I don't know what his problem is, but he shouldn't have taken that out on you. Don't worry about anything ok? I think you are needed down stairs, the caterers are here and need direction. Go do what you do and create a fabulous event ok? Let me worry about the trip."

"Please don't make him angrier. I want him to stay tonight. Maybe he will calm down if we don't bother him."

"I'm not going to bother him, I'm just going to talk to him like a friend and try to get him to be nice to you. The way he just behaved was certainly NOT nice Lena! Now scoot before the caterers light the back yard on fire."

Chapter 3

I don't know what she said to him. But he came out an hour later and said he was able to change his flight and he would leave after breakfast in the morning and we would discuss the details of the trip then.

"You mean I can go? You're ok with it?"

"We will talk about it. But really, I will be having a few busy weeks coming up anyway, so I won't have to worry about commuting home while you're gone, and if I get caught up enough. Maybe we can spend more time together this summer, maybe even take the girls on a trip of some sort. Let's get this party going and talk over breakfast tomorrow. We can go to that little pancake place you like so much ok?"

"Thank you Geoff! Thank you. I love you and can't wait to spend some time with you this summer!"

This time he hugged me back when I went into his arms. I made a mental note to find out what magic Cera used on Geoff to get this response.

"Magic? I haven't talked to Geoffrey yet. What are you talking about?"

"Come on Cera, what did you say to him? He was like a different person! The party is going to begin soon, tell me, how did you get him to come around?"

"Serious Lena, I haven't talked with him. He wasn't in your room when I went in to talk to him. I was looking around for him and saw you two hugging in the back yard and decided not to pursue an argument right then when it looked like you too made up. Serious, I never said a thing to him. I wouldn't lie to you! Never!"

"Well, maybe he realized how awful he had been and was just really sorry. I don't care what happened, I'm just thrilled it did! I'm going to Thailand! Oh my gosh Cera!" I threw myself at her and gave her a hug.

"Down girl, down! You have guests arriving. Go get the girls and let's get this party started!" We were both laughing as we walked up the pathway to greet the guests and get the party started.

The party was a huge success! Even Geoff was having a good time. He was showing off the new car to the neighbor men and I heard him say 'her favorite colors are yellow and purple, no way was I driving anything in those colors' and laughter abound. It was nice to see him enjoying himself and laughing.

This year I hired a DJ instead of a band so the girls would have more music input. The teens were dancing and having a great time! Cera even had me out on the dance floor for a while! The BBQ was phenomenal, the drinks were flowing and everyone was having a great time! After it got dark a group of us went to the back of the house where it was nice and dark and looked at the stars trying to find constellations. None of us really knowing what we were really looking at but making things up and laughing and enjoying the stargazing.

This was definitely the best party yet! I was in such a great mood as I said the last goodbye of the night, I was even feeling hopeful that Geoff and I might make love. Something that hadn't happened in a very long time. Sadly, it was not to be tonight either. When I arrived to bed, Geoff was already there passed out and snoring like a freight train.

"What the hell is that?"

Cera had come out to investigate the racket. "It's Geoff, he always snores like that when he has had too much to drink. Guess I won't be getting lucky tonight huh?"

We both started laughing.

"I think if you want a good night sleep, you better try a different room, I certainly could not sleep with that noise machine going all night! Great party Lena! Really, I'm so glad I was able to be here, it was a blast! Does he appreciate you enough? I think not, you are amazing girlfriend!"

"Thanks Cer! Thank you for everything! Oh my gosh! I'm going to Thailand! I still can't believe it! You are the amazing one! Good night!"

We hugged and went our separate ways. I actually thought about going to another room to sleep, but decided not to rock the boat that was floating on calm seas at the moment. One sleepless night was worth it. I thought anyway.

Chapter 4

Geoff woke me the next morning, later than I thought.

"I overslept, I need to leave in an hour. I have some coffee going. Let's go talk about this trip of yours."

Not exactly the greeting I was hoping for, but he was still here, and willing to talk, so I quickly got up and followed him down to the kitchen.

"So tell me about this trip Cera has promised you."

"Well, we are leaving this coming Friday. She already made arrangements for the girls to fly to Colorado and stay with her sister's family. I thought I would try to arrange some time for them to visit my mom and dad while they are there. I will be gone just over three weeks. I don't know specific details about lodging, but I'm sure Cera will have an itinerary I can e-mail you. She also arranged for a kennel for the dogs, and a house sitter to come check on things around here for us. She really thought of everything. I will e-mail you the house sitter info so you can let them if you will be home. So what do you think?"

"I guess I don't see a reason why not. Have you spoken to your job already I suppose?"

"No, I haven't. I will need to go in Tuesday and talk to them. A lot of what I do can be done from home though, so if I take my computer, I'm sure I can get some time in and it shouldn't be a problem. I so rarely take time off though; I hope it will be ok."

"Well I need to shower and catch my flight back to the city. If you're sure you want to go and the girls are taken care of, then have fun. I can't see any reason why I would come home at all. Just e-mail the info so I have it. Sorry about breakfast."

He gave me a quick peck on the cheek and disappeared upstairs without another word. That was not what I was expecting to say the least. I was a little stunned by the conversation really. I wanted to be excited, and I was, but I was certainly feeling a bit of a let down by Geoff.

I was about to go ask if he needed a ride to the airport, but he always booked his shuttle rides with his commuter flights these days. He said he got better deals that way. So I instead went about making breakfast for the rest of the household while making a mental list of everything that needed to be done before the trip.

Geoff's ride arrived and was followed by the party supply company to pick up table chairs and canopies. The rest of the day flew by with a flurry of activity. Before I even realized it, it was dinner time. I felt terrible because I had nothing planned. Cera to the rescue. We went out for Chinese.

"I haven't had good Americanized Chinese in eons! Normal sauces, meat and veggies, yum! Nothing like real Chinese food in china, yup, that is what I want!"

The girls and I love Chinese food. We get take out every few weeks. We had a favorite place that was clean and had great table service as well as take out, so we went there. I still had to tell the girls about their trip. I was feeling a bit leery about their reactions.

Turns out that they were much more excited than I thought they would be. They didn't have any activities planned until July and were very excited to see Cera's sister again, though I thought seeing her 16-year-old nephew might be the more exciting thing.

"Well, that's settled then, only one thing left to do!"

Cera likes to make big proclamations and it sounded like she was gearing up for one.

"What is that Cera?"

Jill Edick

"Shopping! We must do some shopping! You cannot go to Thailand in the stuff you wear around the house, and the girls will need plenty of outdoor clothes and shoes! Shoes I say, many new shoes for all!"

Cera is a total shoe whore, I had no doubt we would all end up with at least one full suitcase of shoes before she was done, but she had a point, shopping was certainly a necessity!

We only had a few days and plenty to do. So we got an early start the next morning. The phrase shop 'til you drop was eerily accurate. We were exhausted. However, we were pretty well done with shopping. Which was good after the embarrassing credit card denial I got while trying to make a purchase. I sent Geoff a message right away. He said he would look into it, probably the bank was having computer issues. After that we had to launder everything, then pack. I was right on about the shoes too.

Cera had the girls get several pairs of tennis shoes as well as hiking boots and sandals. She made them wear thick socks and the boots all day Wednesday to break them in a bit. Meanwhile I was sent to a spray tan salon to 'deal with all the white'.

Cera had also arranged for us to fly to Denver with the girls on Thursday so they wouldn't have to fly alone, then our flight would leave Friday out of Denver. I could tell she was excited to go home. Her condo was in Broomfield and she rarely got to go there since she travels so much. Plus, she needed to re-pack herself.

By the time we dropped the dogs at the 'pet hotel' and headed for the airport Thursday we were all tired from the whirlwind of events.

The party was forgotten from my mind. Geoff's behavior about the car, the car itself was even forgotten. Geoff said the credit card was taken care of (with no further explanation given) and have a good trip sent via text. Even that strange goodbye was forgotten once we boarded the plane and took off for Denver.

I couldn't believe it. I was about to live a dream!

Part 2

Follow your Curiosity

Focus on the Present

Live in the Moment

Albert Einstein

Chapter 5

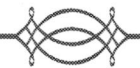

I'm not much of a flyer, I'll be the first to admit it. But that flight into Denver just about made me want to rent a car and drive home and forget the whole trip. Fortunately, the girls are much more tolerant of turbulence than I am and thoroughly enjoyed the flight.

Cera had arranged for a rental car and soon we were off to her condo in Broomfield. She had a small place off the highway which is easy and convenient for her to get to Boulder to see her sister, but was quite a drive from DIA. That said, the drive was beautiful heading west and looking at the stunning Rocky Mountains. I missed Colorado. The state, not so much the life I left behind here or the family. But I couldn't remember the last hike I took, and a feeling of nostalgia took hold and a moment of 'forget the trip, I'm going to stay here and hike' hit me. The desire to get into those mountains and breathe the fresh air that smelled of pine, clean water and pure oxygen was overwhelming. But then I came back to my senses. I remembered that I was about to embark on my dream trip, one that I may never have the chance to experience again. I could always come home to my precious mountains.

"Cera, what is your timeline like for when we fly home? Would we have a few days we can stay here before you have to head out again?"

"Actually, yes. I'm taking some time off this summer. I had hoped I would be starting that time off now, but they talked me into this trip before I take my much needed vacation. I have planned to be off until about mid-July. Of course, that will probably never happen, I will get a call, 'please, please go'. But I should have a couple weeks I would think. Are you thinking of extending this trip a bit?"

I could hear the smile in her voice. I hadn't returned to Colorado in years, and hadn't taken a vacation in years, and nothing without Geoff, unless you count that failed Disney trip.

Jill Edick

"Well I was kind of thinking a hike would be nice. But let's see how I feel after Thailand, and how the girls feel about staying a little longer. Who knows."

We were planning to stay at her place that night and take the girls to Boulder in the morning before we had to head back to the airport. Prudence would have suggested that not drinking too much wine would have been a good idea. But, we were celebrating, I'm not sure what exactly, or perhaps I just forgot, but two bottles of Cera's wine collection disappeared pretty quickly.

Truly

Across the Country:

"Wanna play house?"

"No. I don't. I want to live the dream, MY dream."

Kissing his way down her slender body, capturing a nipple in his mouth and sucking until she gasps. "Soon my beauty. Soon."

An hour passes:

"Just so you know, there is nothing of that bitches that will ever be good enough for me. Nothing."

"Yes princess, you can have whatever you want."

"I want to know you will never cheat on me like you do her."

"Never! How could I?"

"Can it you jerk. You love what I do for you, and for now that's enough. Now shut the fuck up and take me on a trip around the world!"

Chapter 6

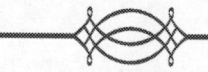

Our early morning was not a great one, but we got the girls up to Boulder.

Cera's sister was exactly as I remembered her. Full of energy and cute as a bug. I felt terrible, I had never met her boys in person. Of course I had seen all their pictures and adventures posted on Facebook. And I chatted with Jena periodically. But reality once again was much grander than pictures. Her boys were now 13 and 16 and looked just like their very handsome dad.

Jena, much like me, believed that whenever she got to see Cera, she should cook for her. There was an enormous brunch laid out for us. It was fun catching up and meeting the boys. Soon enough, it was time for Cera and I to go. After a tearful farewell from the twins, and an 'are you leaving yet' goodbye from Lindy we hit the road.

"I get the impression that as long as Marc is around, Lindy will be very happy to stay." Cera was laughing so hard as we drove away I was afraid we might crash. "I mean really, she was totally googly eyed!"

"I too suspect that she will be missing me a little less with him around."

When we got to the airport, my anxiety kicked in. The dread of the flights was getting me very anxious. First we were to land in LA. Not a stop I was particularly looking forward to, but at least it was still in the US. Next stop was Seoul. Now I'm not saying it's not a lovely place, but that whole North Korea scary mess made this stop right next door not so exciting. Fortunately, it is a quick plane change and off again to Bangkok. I set my watch to Denver time so I would know when I could call the girls once in a while. The time change was 11 hours. Somewhere in all that flying I was going to lose half a day! I'm pretty sure I had a panic attack before I ever got on the plane. Thank goodness Cera is so seasoned at traveling. If left to my own devices, I would never have gotten on that plane.

After so many hours and time zones and minor panic attacks later, we arrived in Bangkok. What a different world. The airport was even different, beautiful, but different. I had never seen dragons in a US airport before, but they were beautiful. The building kind of reminded me of a tunnel, it was very cool. The energy in the air was not one of excited vacationers, but rather business travelers, and natives coming and going. Of course there were many vacationers, but certainly nothing like the mess that was LAX with all the Disney t-shirts and ears and screaming kids, uhg, I much preferred this brand of vacationer. I felt kind of like I had stepped through a time warp, or perhaps not a time warp so much as a space warp. In a way I had. I was absolutely in awe, and we were still in the airport! I could not wait to get to our resort and rest up. I was ready to site see and explore!

We had a car waiting for us complements of Cera's business. We had a bit of a drive out of town to the beach town of Hua Hin. It was amazing. Nothing like I ever imagined, but not a disappointment by any means. I was not even aware that such beautiful beaches and resorts existed in Thailand. It was like being in the Caribbean with the beautiful flowers and palm trees everywhere, and the white sand beaches. How very wrong Geoff had been about the orient. This was truly spectacular.

"Oh Cera! I can't wait to get out and explore! Have you been here before?"

"I have not been here before. This will be new for me too. I did a bunch of research since this will be a mini vacation for me as well, so I have plenty of options of things for us to do. Personally, I like to take the first day and deal with jet lag by lounging by a pool whenever possible. But tomorrow, let's get those walking shoes ready, I have tons of things for us to see and do!"

Our resort was something straight out of a travel magazine. It was incredible. The rooms were gorgeous with views that took your breath away. I liked the idea of sitting by the pool and relaxing. The pool was huge and they had an infinite pool. I had never even seen one in person before. This was a luxury I had never experienced. I was snapping pictures left and right. I kept waiting for the jet lag to hit. I did not have to wait long. We found chairs under a large umbrella and soon we were both dozing. The staff was so amazing they kept the umbrella turned so we wouldn't get burned in the sun.

When we woke up late that afternoon we were starving.

"So, this will be the start of your foreign food education Miss Lena!"

I was a bit afraid, but so hungry that I was ready for anything.

The resort had several restaurants and we chose the most American looking place. I had what I hoped was a hamburger, it was quite good but I don't want to know what it was if not hamburger. The vegetables were amazing, and of course there was plenty of rice and wine. For my first 'Asian' food, I was totally happy and stuffed. Not to mention ready to go to bed.

Cera insisted that we stay up for a while though and we walked through the resort and along the beach. The night view was spectacular. Lights from nearby cities blinking off the water and the beautiful stars in the sky. It took my breath away.

Soon enough we were both walking asleep and decided to retire for the night. I only got a few hours of sleep though before I woke up fully awake and ready to go. I made a cup of coffee and sat on the balcony until Cera came knocking.

"So, I have broken things to do into two lists. First are things we should see, just because it would be a shame to come to Thailand and not see them. But also places I know we both will enjoy. The second list consists of places and things to see and do that us crazy girls want to do and would do no matter what country we are in. I'm also working on a list for you of activities to do in Bangkok and Chiang Mai while I'm working. I will give you that list and some website to check out, but once we get to the other hotels, we can check with concierge for excursions and stuff."

She handed me the list and I was ready to go. We decided we wanted to check out the local markets, but thought we would wait to explore the Night Market. Cera had a car to get us around town, so we put the market on the list for that evening. We wanted to tour the city and check out some of the local history. We booked a tour through the resort and we got to tour the historical areas of the city. I never knew there was so much history here. The architecture was outstanding. I was so glad we did the tour. We went to several temples. The statues were striking. Our guide was knowledgeable about all the statues and their significance. After many pictures of temples and art we went to the Ratchamivet Mareukhathaiyawan palace. That was extraordinary and exotic. It was not what you think of as a 'palace' especially after watching so many specials on the British Royalty. I learned so much about the royals here and the turbulent relationship Thailand had with other countries because of their beliefs. It was an interesting tour. I knew many things about Thailand, but never in a million years did I ever expect some of the things I learned and saw that day.

At the end of the tour, we returned to the resort. Cera insisted on a more traditional dinner that evening before we headed out to the night market. When you think Thai, please do not be confused with 'American Thai'. Although I too love good Thai back home, there just isn't anything that compared to the meal we had that night. We had an assortment of fish and vegetable with our rice. I think I even ate a flower or two. It was delicious. I completely enjoyed our dinner, even though I was unsure what everything was that I just ate.

"I think we need to take a cooking class tomorrow, I want to know what I'm eating, and bring some of this delightfulness back home to the girls!"

Cera laughed at me. "Cooking class, I think I saw something like that at the concierge's desk earlier. We will check that out!"

I'm sure Cera being the restaurant aficionado was not thrilled but she was smart enough to know I would cook her some delicacy the next time she was in town if she did this. Regardless of her reasoning she agreed, I was super excited.

"Alright girl, what says you about hitting the Night Market? I was thinking about not driving, but rather renting a Tuk tuk for the evening."

"A Tuk tuk? What?"

"Oh this will be fun! Let's go, there is a taxi stand out front. Tuk tuk what! Phttt!"

Learn I did. I had seen pictures of these little cart looking things, but did not know their name. It was like a motorcycle with an open multiperson seating area behind it. They were very colorful and thankfully motorized. I can't imagine being the poor person who would have to pedal with two or more people behind them. We found a few others that were headed to the market and we shared the tuk tuk. I was a bit worried about getting back to the resort, but when we were dropped off, I saw there were many of these little 'taxis' and we should be able to get back easily enough.

As I stood looking around, what I saw made me feel stupid for marveling at the tuk tuk so much, it was an enormous market. Lights everywhere, sights and sounds and the smells! The food smelled to amazing wafting from all directions. I instantly regretted eating so much at dinner. I just stood there staring. Why didn't we have things like this in America? This was amazing.

"Hey, Lena, Hello? Are you in there?"

"I'm here, wow, where do we even start? I'm overwhelmed. I have never seen anything like this before."

"Other countries are amazing. We are so stuck up in the US, we forget that the rest of the world is so cool. Now you get why I don't mind the travel so much. Disney is fine, Cruises are nice, but this is real."

"Yes, real. Amazing."

Cera laughed at me and grabbed my hand. "Let's shop, why are we just standing here?"

I could have walked the market all day. Besides the food stands, there were flowers all over. Household items and of course touristy things as well. There was so much to see and little shops tucked into corners to look at. I knew I wanted to come back here every night.

I bought several things to take home to the girls. I wished I had someplace to cook, there were so many amazing things to buy I would love to try in recipes. I wish I had a note pad with me to take notes of some of the delicacies here so I could look for them when I returned home. I hoped after a cooking lesson that I would know what some of this was and what to do with it.

We were in a flower booth cooing at the beautiful orchids when I first noticed 'him'. Cera and I were both marveling at the spectacular flowers and contemplating buying them all for our room when I felt a nudge from behind.

"Excuse me Miss."

He was absolutely the most beautiful man I had ever seen. I was completely speechless. I must have looked like a total idiot because I just stood there gapping at him moving my lips like a goldfish in its bowl unable to speak.

He smiled at me and went on his way.

"Smooth Lena, real smooth. You act like you have never been bumped into by a hunk before."

"Shut up Cera. He wasn't a hunk, he was wow, just wow."

"Wow indeed. Did you even notice his ass or that he has on a prosthetic leg, or were you to busy sharing your impression of a gold fish to notice anything but his face?"

"Nope, face only. But with a face like that, he could be a robot from the neck down and I wouldn't care."

"Well, since you were ignoring everything but his face, let me tell you about that ass, that ass could stop traffic in the middle of Manhattan in rush hour and no one, male or female would mind. You can hear the birds sing when you look at that ass."

"Dammit, I missed that?! Let's follow him!"

"Lena! I'm just shocked at you. Perhaps we should stick to the flowers and get back to a tuk tuk before you get yourself or both of us in trouble."

I looked around again in hopes of catching another glimpse of this mystery Adonis. Alas he was gone.

We picked out several bouquets of flowers and potted orchids and started to leave the market. We were standing at the taxi stand when out of the corner of my eye, I saw the flames of strawberry blonde hair. It was Adonis himself standing not ten yards in front of the taxi stand. I nudged Cera but she had already seen him too.

"Look down this time, I promise you won't regret it!"

Look I did. And was she ever right. All sounds of the city ceased, waves crashed in my ears and I swear I heard the Pina Colada song start playing somewhere. I was staring so intently, that when he turned and I looked up at his face again, it was to my horror that I realized he had caught me so rudely ogling him. He smiled so big that his perfect white teeth literally shone in the night lights. He lifted a hand in a little wave my direction. I looked over at Cera.

"Oh no honey, that wave isn't for me."

I looked at him a gain and he was chuckling. He waved again and then stepped into the street to get into a car that had just pulled up.

"Wow, did you see that car?"

"Car?" I was still feeling a little dazed.

"Earth to Lena! He just got into a custom Mercedes, like the kind only the very rich drive. Only he wasn't driving, he has a driver, you know like the filthy rich have. In this part of the world, that is pretty shocking. If he's from around here, he is well known and he is very very wealthy!"

It was our turn to get in a tuk tuk. As I got seated and put down my purchases I saw the car Cera had seen. It looked like a small limo. Sleek and beautiful, much like the rider.

"Phew! I think I need a drink to celebrate seeing such a marvelous site!"

We both started laughing.

I took a long walk on the beach when we got back to the resort hoping that it would help me wind down so I could rest. Cera had booked an excursion for the next day and a cooking class for that evening and I wanted to be rested up good for it. But try as I might, I could not seem to calm down.

I went back to my room and drank a glass of wine while sitting in my bed staring out at the gorgeous night sky. I finally dozed off. But I awoke from the most intense dream I can ever remember having. I don't particularly remember what it was about, but I knew it had to be pretty erotic, and I was pretty sure I knew who stared in it. But then a huge rush of guilt washed over me. I pictured Geoff in my mind, and felt terrible. Here I was, in Thailand for two days and I was dreaming of another man and hadn't thought about my husband once. What a terrible wife I was.

I grabbed my phone. I knew Geoff would be asleep more than likely, so I sent an email saying I loved and missed him. I also sent messages to the girls with a few pictures attached. The twins had each emailed me a couple of times. Lindy only once. She was having a blast with Marc. Of course she was. The twins reported that she was with him all the time, it was disgusting. I laughed and cried reading these messages.

I was feeling better and managed to get a little more sleep before hurricane Cera came blasting into my room to announce it was time

Jill Edick

for coffee! She must have found a coffee shop somewhere because she put a latte into my hand and it was fabulous.

"Now Lena, how is the most annoying early bird I know still in bed? Get up silly, we leave in an hour for our Elephant Trekking Tour! Wear jeans, I don't care how hot it is."

That caught my attention, Elephant trekking tour, that was not what I was expecting. I guess that is what you get when you let someone else plan your trip. At least it wasn't a horse trek, horses and I have a mutual I don't like you relationship. I hoped Elephants and I got along better.

"Elephants?"

"Yes, I decided if you're going to make me cook, you're getting that narrow ass of yours up on an elephant. Don't look so scandalized. We are going to do something that I think will blow your mind tomorrow, so get moving lazy bones!"

Out blew the hurricane as fast as it blew in. I decided if I was spending time on an elephant, a shower could wait until I got back, so I stayed in bed and enjoyed my latte a while longer.

When I met Cera in the lobby to meet the tour bus for our excursion I had jeans on and ponytail up, sunscreen slathered and another cup of coffee down. I hoped I was ready for this little adventure.

It took a while to get used to the whole elephant thing, but I am happy to report that unlike the last horse I was on, the elephant did not take off at a dead run and scare the bejesus out of me. The worst part was really the flies, and the heat, and the smell, well ok, so it was better than a horse, that's all.

I was doing fine until we approached a river and I thought great here is where we turn around, yay. But oh no, those elephants went right into the river and across we went. Had I previously mentioned I don't swim? I like a nice shallow pool and hot tubs, but swimming in a river, not so much. I looked at Cera on her elephant and sent her a dagger glare. She laughed at me and snapped a picture. She must really hate cooking to torture me this way.

I was in for a surprise though. Once across the river, we went to a Pineapple farm. That was totally surprising. I had never seen pineapple anywhere before but the produce department at the grocery store. We got a tour of the farm and even got to purchase some fresh pineapple. It was delicious. They even made their own wine with pineapple. Cera and I stocked up on that too. I was almost ready to forgive Cera when we had to get back on the elephants for the return to civilization. She was so going to pay. We would be the first to arrive at class and last to leave!

The long hot shower I took upon our return was heavenly. Positively heavenly. I stayed in the shower until I was pretty sure I was a total prune.

Part of the cooking class was dinner. We made our own. I learned the proper technique for preparing a variety of fish and vegetables. I also learned how to cook rice that did not come from a box labeled minute rice or uncle bens. We also made a traditional Thai dessert and tea. It turned out beautifully and very edible. Even Cera's, and she normally couldn't boil water. I bought a cook book and a rice cooker. I also ordered a huge variety of teas to be shipped home.

It was as I was paying that my credit card declined again. I was immediately suspicious. Why would it decline? Because I was in Thailand? Geoff said he took care of the card, surely he notified them I was traveling. I was so embarrassed that Cera had to come to my rescue. I had brought money with me from my personal savings but it was in the room. I promised to pay her when I got up there.

"You better hang onto it, your card seems to be a bit temperamental. Did you bring another card with you?"

I had brought another with me, but it was one Geoff didn't like me to use. It was an emergency card only. We had it so if I was out somewhere and the car broke down I could get towed and repaired quickly. I had never used it. But I kept it with me always. I also put my paychecks from work into a saving account as my pay was not needed for household expenses. I used that money for holidays or to get something special once in a while. I had quite a bit saved and brought most of It with me on the trip so Geoff wouldn't get angry about credit card charges. I was confused about the currency exchange rates though and had used very little of the cash. I figured once the credit card bill came I could pay it with the cash, but that didn't look possible now.

When I got to my room I opened my e-mail. Nothing from Geoff. So I sent him another message and told him about my day and the card issue again, asking him to look into it. The twins had sent me messages again still complaining about Lindy and Marc. They caught them kissing just this morning. I laughed, but was a bit shaken by this news as well. I didn't want anyone to get hurt, and at the end of the trip Lindy was going back to PA. I shot a quick e-mail to Jena to make sure she was aware of the happenings. I responded to the twins and sent Lindy a message too.

Cera showed up about then with a bottle of the pineapple wine and two glasses. We sat on the balcony and enjoyed the wine and each other's company. She showed me pictures of me on the elephant and we laughed.

"So what are we doing tomorrow?

"Well, since I tortured you with elephants today I thought we could go for bit of a hike tomorrow. Wear your swim suit under your clothes."

She got up and walked out before I could even respond. I loved hiking though and was thrilled at the idea.

The wine did its job and I fell right to sleep and no dreams came to me that night.

Nor did a response from Geoff about the card, or anything for that matter.

Chapter 7

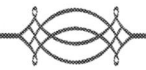

Across the World:

"What's going on? The news, it's wrong isn't it?"

"Don't panic. Things are under control."

"Under control? Where is the money then? Huh?! Where is my money? What about my family? Friends?"

She pushes him away from her.

He slaps her and she falls.

"I said don't fucking panic!"

She tastes blood in her mouth, stands up and gets in his face.

"Fix it mother fucker! I want my money. Get me my money!"

"You're about to get more then that bitch!"

They fall together in a violent sexual act that finishes the argument.

I got up at my usual early time and made coffee and grabbed a newspaper. It was a wall street journal, albeit about 2 days old, but better than nothing I guess. However, it did have some shocking news. The market was being rocked by scandal. Apparently some new insider trading mess. No names were mentioned. But I figured this must be what had Geoff to distracted to respond to me. Any time there was a scandal he worked twice as hard to calm clients and not lose money.

I sent him another message and said I just read about the trading issues and I hoped he was doing alright. I hoped to hear from him soon. I ended with an I love you and sent it off.

Cera showed up about 10 minutes later and immediately hit my coffee pot.

"Pineapple wine sure is good, but damn I have a headache today! I feel like an elephant sat on my head."

She looked like hell too. I didn't feel bad and I drank as much as she did. I hoped she wasn't getting sick.

"You don't look to up to a hike today. Why don't we reschedule it for tomorrow and just hang by the pool today?"

"No way, we are going to that waterfall if it kills me."

"The way you look it just may. Wait, what waterfall?"

"We are going to Pa La-U Waterfall today. It's supposed to have an amazing view of Thailand and Burma at the top and a fabulous pool to swim in. We are going. Besides, I thought tomorrow we could go to the Panee Butterfly Gardens and if we have time a boat ride on the Khlon Koe Daeng."

"Cera, that all sounds great, really, but you don't look great."

"We are going! I just need more coffee."

When we went down to catch our excursion bus though, she was not just needing more coffee. She was a mess.

"OK, I don't think I should go, but you are. It's hiking and a waterfall. You have to go! Just stick with the group here and take tons of pictures for me."

"Oh Cera, I don't mind staying really."

"Stay and do what, watch me sleep off whatever this is? I'll be fine tomorrow, just need some rest. You go and have a blast."

The people we had shared a tuk tuk with the other night were there and stepped up.

"We are on this tour as well, you can hang out with us. It will be fun."

I reluctantly left on the tour leaving Cera behind. I felt guilty as heck until we arrived at the park to start the hike and I met our guide.

Our hiking guide was Adonis himself. All six feet of him shining in the sun. In shorts and boots and prosthetic leg. Wait, he was our guide? Had Cera known? Wait, prosthetic leg, hiking? I was not the first person to notice and apparently question it.

"Hello everyone! I'm Kendall. I will be your guide today. This is truly a spectacular hike and I can't wait to take you all on it. Please let me know if anyone has any medical conditions I should know about and as we start our hike today let me know if we need to slow down the pace at all. Are we about ready to tackle this hike then?"

I was mesmerized. His voice was a fabulous as the rest of him. I detected an accent but could not place it. English perhaps? I was not sure. He caught my eye and winked.

"Before we start, I like to make sure everyone has a hiking buddy. Your buddy will be your second set of hands, and believe me there are spots on the trail that another set of hands is nice. Also we help each other a lot. So I think everyone is in pairs except one? I believe we had a drop out just this morning leaving us with a single, so I will be Darlena's buddy today. All righty, everyone get with your buddy and Darlena if you could please come on up here with me."

Well, my inner goldfish took over at that moment. Cera wasn't sick, I knew this without a doubt now. The little twit planned this. How did she know? How did this happen. I was standing stock still in a state of shock when I hear beside me "I think you must be my buddy Darlena? Are you ready for our hike?"

I never saw or even heard him come up beside me. How was he so stealthy? How was I so oblivious?

I quickly found my voice, "Yes, yes I'm Darlena, please call me Lena."

"Lena, beautiful! Well shall we hike?"

Well, what was I supposed to say to that, Adonis just asked me to hike with him. Like I would turn that down!

So off we went. It was so beautiful. The plants were gorgeous and tall, they obviously thrived in the humidity. The path was mostly wide enough to walk side by side most of the way. Although it wasn't a particularly hard hike, I could tell I hadn't hiked in a while. Fortunately, many of the others with us were obviously not hikers at all, so our pace was nice and easily manageable.

I was still so stunned by the turn of events I could hardly speak. Either Kendall did not notice or was ok with my 'shyness'.

"So Lena, where are you visiting us from?"

"Pennsylvania" I sputtered out not even thinking twice that he would know where that was. Very rude of me.

"I have been. Beautiful state."

He noticed my surprise. "I have traveled quite a lot. I'm an avid climber. I have traveled all over the world looking for the best mountains."

"Wow, you're a climber. How interesting. Are you from Thailand then and just travel?

"My family is in Thailand. I love it here. I was not born here. I was born in Australia where I lived with my mom until I was three. She met my stepdad when he was there on business. They fell in love and this is where I was raised. I have been very fortunate that I have been able to travel and pursue my hobbies. I do my fair share of work; I work for my step fathers company as a buyer. That permits me travel time as well.

When I'm home I pick up odd jobs guiding hikes in the area. I prefer to stay up near Chiang Mai. But I was in Bangkok for business a while ago and decided to stay on here for a few weeks. This is one of my favorite walks in the area."

"How lucky for you. I wish I could travel more. But I have been fortunate to get to come along with my friend on this trip. I am enjoying it immensely."

Some of the tourists were begging for a break behind us.

"Will you be ok waiting here for me while I go check on the others quickly?"

"Of course."

He bound off to check on the others. It was like watching a gazelle. I was going to ask about the leg, but after walking with him and watching him run off to check the others, there was obviously nothing he couldn't do with the prosthesis. He was entirely more capable of this hike than many of the tourists taking it.

Before I knew it he was back and we were off again.

He stopped more frequently now and was pointing out local vegetation and birds as we went. It wasn't too much longer before we got to the first level of falls. It was absolutely breathtaking. Cera was certainly right, I loved waterfalls and I was so glad I came without her on this hike. Although I still felt that there was some master manipulation at play here.

"Ok folks, here is the lowest of the falls. From here on it gets more step. It is totally worth it to get to the top. The views are amazing and there is a wonderful pool up there we can swim in. However, that stretch of hike is not for everyone. If you prefer to stop here, I will get your meals ready for you and leave you to enjoy this beautiful afternoon. For those who wish to continue, I will take you up further and we will meet anyone who chooses to stay on the way back down."

There were a few couples who decided to stay here. I almost couldn't blame them, it was an amazing place to stop and spend a few hours enjoying the day. Kendall whipped his pack off and had lunches and drinks out and passed along quickly. I had forgotten lunch was included and completely surprised that he was carrying all the food and drinks for the whole tour group.

"Wow, that almost doesn't seem fair."

He laughed. "It's alright. Lunch is really nothing more than a sack lunch and bottled water. I carry much more on some of my climbs."

"Where have you climbed at?"

"All over really. The ones you probably would recognize are Mt. McKinley in Alaska, and Everest. I'm hoping to take on K2 in the next year."

"Everest?! My goodness, you climbed Mt. Everest?"

"Yes I did. First one legged man to summit. It was quite an accomplishment."

"I am very impressed. That is an accomplishment most people cannot say regardless of the number of limbs they have."

"Thank you. That is actually a perfect response. Most people don't know what to say and generally look like assholes. So sorry, please pardon my language. I tend to get a bit frustrated when I think of the nonsense people think to say when they see my lack of leg."

"I can only imagine. Would it be wrong to ask how you came to be missing a limb?"

"Not at all. I was in an accident when I was about five. The doctors tried to save my leg and I kept it for several years. But it was intensely painful and I was unable to walk properly or play sports. I decided when I was seven that an amputation would be better than what I had. At least with amputation I could get a prosthetic leg that would allow me to walk without limping. So I did it. Best decision ever. Obviously as I have grown I have needed new prosthesis, but that was still better than what I was living. Now I not only walk and play sports, I'm an avid climber and live my life more effectually than many people I know."

"You are very inspirational Kendall. I feel very honored to have gotten to meet you."

We stopped again.

"Folks, we are about half way, this is the next best stopping spot until we get to the top. Anyone who would like to stop now?"

We lost four more people. That left us with just Kendall, myself and four others.

With the smaller group we were able to travel a bit faster, but Kendall was also able to share more history of the land we were on and the park that we were hiking in.

"We are actually quite lucky today. The weather is being most cooperative. This tends to be our rainy season. It is much more humid now than it will be in a couple of months. But with the rainy weather we get the lush plant life that make this hike so lovely.

We walked on for a while longer and came to an amazing clear blue pool of water with a majestic waterfall landing on its surface.

"Wow, this is breathtaking."

Kendall stood nearby smiling as we all took in the majesty before us.

"We can climb up to the top of the falls, from there you can see Thailand and Burma. Best view in the country. But for now, I will pass out the lunches as I think we have all earned a break. Feel free to jump in the pool for a swim if you like. We will spend about an hour here before we head back to collect the others."

The other two couples collected their lunches and went in different directions to eat and enjoy the day.

Jill Edick

"Well Lena, I guess it's just you and I for lunch. I think I would like to cool off a bit before I eat, care to join me for a swim?"

"Oh, I'm not much of a swimmer, more of a wader. How deep does it get?"

"Pretty deep, come in, if it gets to deep you can stop or I can help you."

He sat down then and took off his leg. He hopped up on his other leg perfectly like this was no big deal. I can't balance on two legs most days, I was a bit jealous of his gracefulness actually.

While I was pondering this, he pulled off his t-shirt. The goldfish returned. I was struck dumb. What a magnificent man. He was simply the most incredible person I have ever seen.

"Do you have your swimsuit on Lena? If not, I can hold a towel for you to change if you like."

I couldn't even comprehend what he just said. I was still staring like an idiot.

"Lena? Are you all right?"

"What? Oh yes, fine. Just admiring the scenery."

As soon as I said it I immediately regretted it and he burst out laughing.

"Well thank, you, I don't believe I have ever been refereed to that way before. Of course if I am being too arrogant and you were actually looking behind me with x-ray eyes, please correct me."

I had to have been 100 shades of red, pink and purple.

"I am so sorry, I'm so embarrassed."

"No need to be embarrassed. Please. About your suit?"

"I have it on, give me just a moment please."

I was absolutely horrified. I took a short walk behind a tree to take off my top and shorts while I tried to gather my wits about me.

When I returned he was already swimming out to the middle of the pool. My gosh was there anything he couldn't do? He swam better than any fish I had ever seen. All I could do was dog paddle gracelessly in circles.

I walked to the edge of the water. It was cool but felt so good in the heat of the day. I slowly walked out a bit further. Very quickly the water was up to my waist. Far enough for me.

"Now Lena, you can come further than that!"

"Oh no, I don't think I will. I have made enough of a jerk of myself today, I don't need to add being rescued to the list."

He swam over to me and stood in front of me putting a hand on my shoulder for balance.

"Rescuing you would be a pleasure. Please, if you have never swum in a water fall, you are missing an experience."

I let him take my hand and pull me out further. Great I thought, this is where I die. In the arms of Adonis while I drowned thinking I could swim under a water fall. Stupid stupid stupid. But forward I went.

Then suddenly there was nothing below my feet and down I went.

I felt a strong arm around my waist and I broke the surface.

"Lena! I'm so sorry, I didn't realize you really could not swim at all. Now it is my turn to be embarrassed."

He pulled me to where I could stand again.

"No, it's ok, I was just surprised. I'm ok. I wanted to swim in the falls, it's ok. Let me just get my breath and we can try again."

Jill Edick

This time we worked our way out and he kept an arm around me the whole time.

"OK, here is where the drop off is. Ready?"

"Sure, let's do this."

He took my hands and floated out on his back pulling me with him. I flutter kicked my feet and together we glided across the pool towards the falls. Soon we were at the base of the falls getting water splashed on our heads.

"Want to go under them?"

"What's on the other side?"

"Let me show you, take a deep breath and hold on Lena."

I did as he said and closed my eyes. He was pulling me under the falls. Then I felt the water stop hitting my head and we stopped moving.

"Open your eyes Lena."

I did. There aren't enough words in the language to express what I was seeing. We were in a cavern behind the falls looking at the back side of the falls. It was like looking at a moving crystal curtain. All noise was shut out except the water hitting itself. The cavern was small but glistened from the water running down the walls. It was like thousands of tiny gems were embedded in the walls. It was so astounding.

"What are you thinking Lena?"

"This is amazing. Thank you Kendall."

He was still holding me while we floated behind the falls. I looked in his eyes and I melted. They were the most sensuous shade of green I had ever seen. And they were staring at me. For a moment I thought he was going to kiss me, for a moment I thought I was going to kiss him. The spell broke when another couple suddenly joined us behind the falls.

Truly

"Well Lena, I think we should go eat some lunch, we will need to go down soon and I still need to take you up to see the view."

We repeated the actions to get out of the cavern and slowly made our way out of the pool. I grabbed my clothes and a towel and went behind my tree and quickly dried off and changed. I was still a bit dazed. Would I have kissed him back if he kissed me? My brain was saying of course not silly, you would have slapped him and swam away. My heart told my brain to shut the hell up, not only would I have kissed him back I may never have left that little cavern again.

"Lena? Are you ok back there?"

"Oh yes." I walked out and he was staring at me again with those eyes. I had to look away for fear my heart would take over and I would find myself in his arms.

He had our lunches out on a blanket. I don't know where that came from but there is was. He was right though, pretty boring sack lunch. Ham sandwich on a hoagie roll, chips and a piece of fruit. There was a chocolate chip cookie in there too, and a bottle of water. The hike was amazing, the pool and waterfall more so. The lunch left much to be desired. I wondered how much Cera had paid for this. Cera! Oh that woman!

"What are you thinking? You have the most expressive face."

I almost choked as I started laughing. "I was just thinking about my friend that took ill so suddenly this morning and couldn't come. I was thinking maybe she was trying to sabotage me."

"Sabotage?"

"Well yes. She doesn't much care for my husband, and I think she might have figured out who was the excursion leader somehow and played sick to push me on you. Sounds like something she would do."

He laughed now too. "Well I am flattered. Why does she not like your husband? And if I may be so bold, where is your husband?"

"He's a stock broker in New York. We don't travel much. He works a lot. He commutes home to Flourtown every few weeks to see us. I guess Cera just doesn't understand our life. Cera travels for work and decided to bring me with her for this trip. I've always wanted to go to Thailand. She's a good friend, perhaps a bit to meddling, but still I know she loves me to I will forgive her. Not until I torture her a bit first though."

"Well I have to agree with Cera. If you were my wife I would never leave your side. Do you have children then?"

"Yes, three. My oldest daughter is 14 my twin girls are 12. They are amazing."

He was frowning, the laughter had left his eyes. I thought he was mad at me for a minute.

"And this man of yours just leaves the four of you alone. For weeks on end. Well, I am definitely in agreement with your friend then. That doesn't sound like a marriage."

My face dropped. My heart sank. I knew how Cera felt, but had never really heard it put to words before. It was crushing.

"My apologies Miss Lena. I should learn to keep my opinions to myself, I am terribly sorry. I did not mean to upset you. Let's have a change of topic shall we. If your done with lunch, I would very much enjoy showing you the best view you will ever see."

My brain said yes great, my heart said dummy, you already saw the best view ever.

He packed up our trash and the blanket and put them in his pack, but left the pack there by the pool.

"I'll pick that upon our way back." He held his hand to me. I hesitated only a moment then took it. Together we walked around the pool and over to a rock outcropped where we had to let go of each other to climb up and over the rocks.

When we got above the waterfall the view knocked the breath out of my lungs. He wasn't kidding about seeing all of Thailand and Burma. Every direction I turned was even more amazing than the last.

"Oh Kendall, this is amazing. No wonder you love this so much. It's like being on top of the world."

"Well it's no Everest, but Everest never had the view I have now."

I turned to look at him and he was staring at me again with his soft silky eyes.

A sigh escaped my lips. Once again I thought I was in trouble when both couples we were hiking with stumbled up the rocks to join us.

"Glad you all could make it up here!" Kendall went over to them and started pointing out cities in Thailand and Burma and started taking pictures for all of us.

Our hike down seemed to go so fast. Too fast. I never wanted to leave. Here I was just Lena, not wife and mom, just me in this stunning place. Living. But all good things must end I've heard. And soon we were down and back on the bus to the resort.

When we returned to the resort Kendall said good byes to everyone and refused all tips offered saying that this was as much for him as them and their thanks was all he needed. I walked up to give him my thanks. He turned to me and without a word pulled me into his arms and kissed me like he meant it. My arms were around his neck in a second and all thoughts of where I was and who I was with left my mind completely as my heart took over and kissed back with a passion I had never felt, really, didn't even know I had.

Behind me the sound of wolf whistles and clapping started up. Suddenly my brain found itself and pulled me back to reality and out of Kendall's arms. I looked up at him and he was grinning ear to ear. I turned and saw the owner of the wolf whistle was none other than Cera.

I mouthed "dead meat" in her direction and she laughed and mouthed back "bring it on".

Suddenly the arm was around me again. I felt something being slipped into my pocket as he stared into my eyes. "Remember what I said, I would cherish you as my wife and would never forsake my children. I loved every minute of our day together Lena. Enjoy the rest of your trip."

He let me go, turned and strode away. I stood there marveling at his perfect gait and chiseled butt. He reached behind him and smoothed the seat of his shorts then threw an ornery smile over his shoulder at me like he just knew I had been staring at his ass so intently.

Cera came up to my side, "So, how was your afternoon?"

"You, you you!! You weren't sick at all! How did you figure out who he was? Why did you do this? I'm married. OH MY GOD! I just cheated on my husband in front of witnesses!!"

"Lena, I know your pissed at the moment, but tell me you didn't just have the best day of your life, tell me and mean it! I told you he would be known and wealthy. It wasn't too hard to figure out who he was, when I was looking at excursions I saw his name on the hike. I decided you deserved a fun day even if it was without me. AND you did not cheat on your husband. You were kissed by a god. Period. You were kissed, that is all. And maybe you enjoyed it. Good! That's the point of a kiss. But that was all. He left and your virtue is intact. Now, I am starving and I want to hear all about your day and see some pictures!"

We found a restaurant and ordered wine as I shared the day with her. We ate and drank ourselves into two bottles of wine. By the time we stumbled up to our room, I had completely forgiven her and myself for the moment. I was actually tempted to send Geoff and email telling him to straighten up and start cherishing me. But fortunately for us both I passed out.

Chapter 8

When I woke the next morning quite hungover, I looked at my computer and opened my e-mail. There was nothing from Geoff. No response to the credit card. No news about the scandal. Nothing. The guilt that had started to creep in immediately went away. I text and e-mail him while he's gone all the time. Why wasn't he even concerned about me and the fact that I may not have any money for all he knows. Had he even called the girls? I looked at the time. I thought they should still be up so I decided to call them.

Laney answered the phone, but Lissa was right there with her.

"Mommy! We miss you! Where are you what are you doing, what time is it?"

"Whoa girls slow down. It's early, I haven't even had coffee yet." Cera walked in then with the magic cups of lattes, (I needed to find that coffee shop) handed me one and sat down.

"I'm in Hua Hin. I sent you a bunch of pictures. Did you see them? Auntie Cece took a cooking class with me the other evening and I hiked to a waterfall yesterday. What are you girls doing?"

They were off. For the next fifteen minutes Cera and I listened to them gush on and on about everything. They went hiking, they bought camping stuff and were going camping this weekend. And they went to the pool and flatirons mall and to the movies. And they had a blue ray player in their room and Lindy spends all her time kissing Marc and Auntie Jena lets them eat macaroni at every meal.

"Well it sounds like you're having a great time. Have you heard from dad?"

Jill Edick

"No, dad hasn't called or texted. But he never does really."

"I'm sorry girls. That's too bad. I miss you though and I have bought you some really cool things! I love you all so much. Is Lindy there I can say hi to her quick?"

A minute later Lindy was there too. She said the brats were liars and not to believe anything they said. Cera and I just laughed. We knew full well from Jena that the twins weren't liars and Marc and Lindy were now under constant supervision whether they knew it or not.

We all chatted for a while longer, then Cera announced it was time for us to leave.

"I love you girls. Have fun and mind Jena."

"We love you mommy! Can't wait to see you. Bye!"

We all hung up.

"So, Geoff doesn't even call them when he's gone? Really Lena, I don't understand. I don't want to start the day in a fight. Let's just get dressed so we can go. It's our last day here, let's go have some fun."

"Cera?"

"Yes?"

"Before we go home, would you do me a favor?"

"Of course, what can I do for you?"

"Tell me. Tell me why you hate Geoff. Please. Not now, I don't think I can hear it right now, but promise me, you will tell me."

"Oh Lena…"

"Please Cer, please. I know it's more than you have told me. You practically threw me at Kendall yesterday. Why would you do that if there wasn't more to how you feel about Geoff."

"All right, all right. I'll tell you, but in my time. I won't promise before the trip is over. I want you to have a great time and not think about Geoff. We will talk before you go home. OK?"

"Yes. Thank you."

"Come on, I have a great day planned. Let's get moving."

We got ready and went out front to catch a tuk tuk. Those were so fun. New York could use these. Not that I went there often, but when I had been it was crazy.

We went to the Butterfly Gardens and it was so cool. I have been to The Butterfly Pavilion back in Colorado, and it was cool, but it was indoors.

Here, we were outdoors, with native plants and insects. The butterflies were everywhere. It was like a combination outdoor butterfly pavilion and botanical garden. It was so humid though that I didn't think I could sit there all day. Were it not so humid, I probably could have spent the whole day there until they kicked me out at closing.

"That was just amazing and so beautiful Cera, did you like it?"

"Of course I did, I'm the science nerd remember! Plants and animals and the environment are my life! I picked up a brochure in the gift shop. There is a palace across the way and they offer tours throughout the day, want to go over and check it out?"

"Sure. You know me and royalty, let's go."

The palace was the Klai Kangwan Palace. It was very cool. More what I would have thought of as a Spanish style than Thai style. The exterior was beautiful but did not make me think royal. We registered for a tour. Inside was a different story. Definitely more what you would think of a royal palace in Thailand. Many beautiful statues and Buddha's. Simply magnificent. We did not get to see the private residence, but based on what we were seeing the private quarters must be quite opulent.

"Well that was pretty cool too. I admit, I never really understood your fascination with the Royals until now. We have found some great places to visit today. Are you up for that boat ride now?"

"Oh dear, you know me and water Cer."

"Oh give that up. You swam in a mountain pool under a waterfall with Mr. Hunk, you can ride in a boat with me."

"Yeah, well, he held on and promised to rescue me. What ae you offering? Huh?"

We both broke up in laughter. I was fighting a losing battle and knew it. But the boat ride did sound intriguing anyway.

We got a tuk tuk to the docks and the driver knew English and helped us find a boat driver and got us a deal on the ride. Cera tipped him well and told him she would double it if he came back to pick us up. Being down by the docks was a bit more unnerving than other places we had been. It wasn't a big tourist area and most of the people here did not speak English. The driver agreed to come get us in an hour and a half, and we got in the boat and were off.

We had a lot of fun seeing the city from the water and watching the fishermen at work. It was actually quite fascinating. Our captain did know a little English and we were able to communicate and understand some of his stories. We were having a very pleasurable time. But then the weather decided to take a turn and we finally got a feel for the rain in Thailand. Our boat went back to the dock quickly. I was surprised but very happy our tuk tuk was there. He got us back to the resort in short order and Cera gave him a very generous tip.

We went in and dried off before heading down for dinner. By the time dinner was done, the rain was done as well, leaving a beautiful but extremely humid night before us. We decided to sit out by the pool and share a few drinks under the stars.

"Do we really have to leave this place tomorrow?"

"Ha! This is only the first place you get to see. If you love it this much, how will I ever get you out of the country?"

"Do we have to leave the country?"

"I think the girls would like me to return their mom, so yes. I can't tell you how happy I am that you are having such a good time though. You deserve it Lena. Never forget that! You deserve fun too!"

"Thank you Cera. I will never be able to repay this. You are such a great friend. What did I do to deserve you?"

"You need me. And I need you. You take care of me and you were my friend when others wouldn't be. You stood by me through thick and thin. Let's just consider this repayment and own that we are both amazing friends and we deserve another drink!"

"I'll drink to that!"

We were both laughing and having fun when Cera announced we should stop drinking like 20 somethings and get some sleep.

"I'm the mom here, I'll decide when we have had enough.""

"Yes mom, whatever you say mom."

"Good! On that note, off to bed with us."

The way we were laughing as we stumbled to our rooms, I felt sure the hotel would be happy to get rid of us. But I really didn't care, I was having the time of my life!

Chapter 9

I was up of course when Cera came bursting in clad in her bikini and sun hat.

"What are you doing Cera? I thought we were leaving this morning."

"We are, but we don't have to check out here until 11 and we can't check in until 3:00 in Bangkok. So I figure the weather is nice, I'm packed and ready to go, let's go catch some sun shine for a while longer. Hurry hurry, times a ticking."

Out she blew. It's times like these that I wonder why she doesn't consider herself a morning person. I changed into my suit and met her at the pool where she had ordered us a huge breakfast. I have to admit, I hated to leave, but since I had to, leaving in style was just the way to do it.

At 10:30 we reluctantly got up to change and check out. Soon we were on the road to Bangkok.

"We will have some time to kill, so I thought we could check out a market or temple while we wait. Any thoughts?"

"Let's hit another market. That was fun."

She stopped at a gas station and picked up a map and a recommendation for the Thanon Khoa san market and we were off again. It didn't take long to find the market, but parking was another story. We ended up walking some ways but it was worth it.

This was the tourist market if ever there was one. I bought tons of souvenirs for the girls and two new bags for myself to carry everything in. We had a great lunch. We both tried several new things way out of our comfort zone and actually enjoyed them. We shopped so long we

Truly

didn't even realize until lights started popping on that we could go get checked into our hotel.

I hoped I could come here again before we left, but I had said that before. I knew that once again as much as I was loving this, there was certainly bound to be something just as great to see tomorrow.

As we were walking back to the car, a sleek black Mercedes drove past. Suddenly it braked, and out of the moon roof stood Kendall.

"Hello ladies! Can I give you a lift somewhere?"

Cera looked at me and whispered, "would you like to ride with him? The car is right here, I don't need a ride, but perhaps you would like to go for a ride." She was winking at me and had a most mischievous grin on her face.

"Your evil Cera." I turned away from her. "Hi Kendall! I think we are ok, the car is right here. Thank you though!"

He looked disappointed, but then suddenly his face brightened and he pulled himself out of the moon roof and jumped down in front of us.

"So, you two have moved on to Bangkok huh? Can I suggest any places to visit while you're here?"

"I'm not even sure how long we are here or where we are going next. We are here for Cera's business. I'm just tagging along. Cera, how long will we be here?"

"I'm genuinely sorry to say only tomorrow. We leave day after for the Chaing Mai area. That's where we will be spending the rest of our time."

"Are you working tomorrow Cera? If you are I would be happy to accompany Lena around the city." He turned to me, "If you would like the company shall I say."

"I am working tomorrow. I would feel much better if Lena had some company, I would hate for her to end up in a bad part of town alone. Lena, what do you think?"

"Oh, um, I, uh, sure. Company would be nice. Thank you."

"Excellent! What hotel shall I pick you up at?"

Cera gave him our hotel name and told him I'm the earliest riser she has ever met. She had to be to work by 8:00.

"Perfect! How about I pick you up at 7 and I take you out for breakfast?"

"Great, Thank you Kendall. Please don't feel like you have to do this if you have your own business to attend to."

"This is the only business I have. I will see you in the morning Lena." He grabbed my hand and kissed it. Smiled at Cera and ducked into the car, this time using a door.

I turned to Cera. She was still wearing that evil cat ate the canary grin. "You evil woman! How could you do that to me!"

"Do what? Give you something to do tomorrow that will be safer than roaming on your own?"

"Safer? Safer? Are you kidding, he looks at me like I'm lunch!"

"Well maybe you should wear some bread tomorrow and enjoy it!"

She turned from me and got into the car. I wasn't even sure how to respond to that. Had she really just suggested I cheat?

"Hey, Lena, hellllloooooo? Are you going to get in this car? I'm ready to eat some of the goodies we bought and drink some wine. Let's go."

I got in the car and stared at her.

"Are you going to speak or just stare daggers at me? Remember I'm driving in a foreign land and you should not kill me."

"What are you thinking?"

"I'm thinking that you deserve some fun, lord knows your 'husband' doesn't skimp on fun. Kendall is great. He obviously thinks your great, and what the hell, what happens in Bangkok stays in Bangkok."

"What do you mean my husband doesn't skimp on fun? He works all the time and when he has a spare moment he is home with us."

"Sure Lena, keep telling yourself that. Listen, this isn't the time for this conversation. I just want you to have fun and enjoy this trip. Kendall is gorgeous and will keep you safe in this city where you could easily get into trouble by yourself. Think of him as a tour guide/body guard for the day and let it go where it may. OK? Look we are here, and you didn't even enjoy the sights while we were driving."

Cera got out of the car and handed keys over to the valet while a bell hop was unloading our luggage. I guess that conversation was over. I got out and followed her into the hotel.

"I think we are sharing for the next two nights. But I will have a suite again so we will have our own rooms again in Chiang Mai."

"You know I'm ok sharing. I feel like I have been a terrible friend and guest. I haven't even thanked you for all of this. Thanks Cera. Really, I am having fun and I appreciate all you have done. I don't think I will dress as bread tomorrow and be a stranger's lunch, but the idea is certainly delicious. First round on me tonight!"

"Yes, my Lena is back. And you have thanked me, so relax and enjoy. I'm thrilled to have been able to give you this. Now let's check out these accommodations and enjoy some cuisine!"

Enjoy we did. I bought the first bottle, and we smartly stopped at that tonight. Of course my credit card declined again, but I had exchanged some of my cash for baht and it was good. I was still quite upset about the card though. So before I went to bed I tried calling Geoff. He did not answer so I left a voice mail and sent an email as well. I was horrified at the thought of being out tomorrow and having my card reject while with Kendall. I decided I better exchange a bit more money in the morning.

Chapter 10

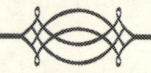

I was impressed, Cera actually got up and moving by 6 the next morning. She even had coffee going. I did not know she knew what dawn looked like, but miracles never ceased to happen or amaze.

"I'm done in the bathroom. Go get gorgeous for your tour today. I'm going to head out and grab a bite to eat before meeting with my work compadres. I hope to be back by dinner time, but do not rush back on my behalf. Remember, I live in hotels in foreign places for a living, I will be good. As a matter of fact, come in late. I insist." She gave me a quick hug a wink and blew out the door.

I jumped into the shower and quickly got ready. I headed down to the concierge to exchange some more money, but was stopped on the way. Kendall was already here.

"Good morning beautiful. Are you ready for some breakfast?"

"Good morning Kendall. I was just going to exchange some cash, give me just a minute."

"No need, today is on me, let's go shall we?"

I wasn't given any time to resist, he grabbed my hand and pulled me out of the hotel.

I was expecting to see the Mercedes, instead, parked on the sidewalk in front, was a motorcycle. Kendall handed me a helmet.

"Um, we are on that?"

"Yeah. I love riding. And I can't think of a better way to see the city. Since I only have one day to show you the whole thing, I thought, why not. So I rented a motorcycle and here we go."

He put on his helmet and got on the bike kicking it to life. I had never ridden on a motorcycle before and was freaking out. He just smiled at me and pulled me on behind him.

"Just hold on Lena, you'll be fine."

"What do I hold on to?"

"Well me of course!"

He pulled my arms around his waist, and started to pull away from the hotel.

He was absolutely right about seeing the city this way. It was great having a complete view of everything without the hindrance of car doors and a roof in the way. At first I thought it was just like any other large city, but as we drove on, little markets were cropping up down streets and we started passing temples and sculpture parks. Though still a big city like many others, it was definitely not like home.

We pulled over at what looked like a little diner. Kendall again parked on the sidewalk. He turned a little and took my hand to help me climb off then followed. He put our helmets on the handle bars and took my hand.

"This is one of my favorite places in all of Bangkok. It doesn't look like much, but trust me when I say, best food ever."

We walked in and it was definitely what I call a hole in the wall diner, however the smells were heavenly.

Kendall was immediately greeted and started having a conversation in what I assumed was Thai. He turned to me and in perfect English introduced me and the lady he had been talking to as Mama Xu. She greeted me in broken but still clear English. "It about time he bring nice girl in here. You American, you like coffee?"

"Yes please, thank you."

Kendall led me to a tiny booth and the lady he had been talking to brought over two cups of coffee. "I know what Kenny want, what I get for you miss?"

"Oh, I don't know, do you have a menu?"

"No menu, I bring you American breakfast, you like."

She bustled away and I looked at Kendall.

"So Kenny, what can I expect to get? I'm a bit nervous."

He burst out laughing. He grabbed my hands from across the table.

"Ah, Kenny is a name reserved for my elders, primarily because I respect my elders completely and they can call me what they want. But, please, no Kenny. I feel 5 when someone calls me that. As far a breakfast goes, I'm sure it will be great. Mama Xu is a fabulous cook and very knowledgeable about cultural foods. You won't get bacon, but I bet you get some sort of sausage and eggs, probably a traditional Thai biscuit but it will have a fruit spread of some sort for you crazy Americans." He continued to chuckle.

I took a drink of my coffee and I have to admit it was the best I'd had been served since I arrived in Thailand.

"So tell me, how did you find this place and how do you know the owner?"

"My step-fathers company sells products to her. I have known her since I first arrived over here and my step-dad started to bring me with him to do client visits. I know many little places like this all over the country. Of course my step-dad is a smart business man. He also sells to many resorts across the country. That's how I know many of those places as well and have been given jobs as tour guides periodically. It allows me the chance to get in the hills, and gives the regular guides a much needed break. And I can conduct business as well. It's great for everyone."

"What is your step father's business?"

"He is one of the primary agriculture suppliers here in Thailand. He used to have the largest rice paddies in Thailand. He has since sold many acres of the rice paddies as he expanded into more of an animal based product. He has an extensive chicken business, and buffalo business. He used to raise the buffalo primarily to sell for farming, but as tourism grew in Thailand and western tourist specifically, a need for red meat became greater. So he expanded his buffalo business. He still sells the males for farming, but the females are being sold to use for meat products to many restaurants and resorts. He keeps a large breeding stock that gets rotated regularly. I do much of the buying of new stock from other countries to keep our breed pure. I also do a lot of quality control at our buyer's places of business. Chances are if you had beef products or chicken product while in Hua Hin, it probably came from one of our farms. Odds are the rice you have eaten either came from us or one of the farms we previously owned."

"Wow. That is very impressive."

Our food arrived right then. It appeared we were being given the same thing.

Kendall spoke first. "Pancakes! I have not had those since I traveled to the America's last. When did you start making these?"

"I made special for your girl Kenny. Want to impress her for you."

He started laughing. "Well thank you so much. I know I am very impressed."

She walked away smiling.

"Wow, it's like I'm in a little diner in Pennsylvania. Eggs, sausage, pancakes. Certainly not what I was expecting."

"Well let me know what you think of that sausage. I promise it's not what you think it is. Pork isn't a real big thing in these parts. I bet that is one of our buffalo there. I know those are our eggs. All organic, free range. Enjoy."

Enjoy I did. I had never had sausage like this before. But it was amazing. Typically, not a sausage person, this converted me. I never needed pork sausage again after eating this. I wondered if I could wrangle a recipe out of her. Perhaps if I gave her a recipe for pancakes. They were good, but my homemade pancakes knocked these ones out. I shared this thought with Kendall.

"Ha! No I would not offer a trade. I don't want her offended even if I agree. But I bet she would be honored to share her recipe with you, if there is a recipe. If you give me that pancake recipe of yours though, I will see that it gets slipped into her next shipment."

We devoured the breakfast. When we were done Mama Xu came over and Kendall asked for the sausage recipe on my behalf. She started beaming and grabbed a napkin. She spent five minutes writing an elaborate recipe on the napkin. I thanked her profusely.

When she left I handed it to Kendall. "I presume you can translate this for me?"

"Nope, I cannot. My mastery of the language is limited to spoken only. However, my mother should be able to handle the translation. I guess I will just have to meet you in Chiang Mai to get you the translation."

"Hmm, why do I feel like you and Cera are in cahoots?"

"I don't know about Cera, but I will do whatever it takes to get you behind me on a bike again and again. Speaking of, shall we hit the road? First stop, get you a backpack. I don't like having that bag of yours between you and I on the bike."

It was my turn to laugh. "Well I just bought a new backpack yesterday actually. Had I known..."

We started riding towards a little shop where he told me to wait with the bike. He came back a minute later with a small backpack. He took

Truly

my purse from me and put it in the back pack which he put on my shoulders. Every touch sent shivers down my spine. How was I going to get through this day?

We climbed back on the bike and he pulled me up close to him and wrapped my arms around his waist again. A small sigh escaped my lips. "I heard that." Then he started the bike and we were off.

He turned slightly over his shoulder so I could hear him, "I'm taking you to the old city. I thought we could go to Grand Palace and a couple of temples there. There is also a great market there I thought we could walk through if time permits. I also booked a dinner cruise for this evening."

"Dinner too? Wow you have a full day planned for me."

"Well I got the impression that Cera wouldn't mind."

"I do believe you got the correct impression." I gripped him a little tighter around his waist. It was his turn to let a growl escape. I laughed softly in his ear.

I was feeling like a school girl who just snuck out of her bedroom window after curfew to ride on the motorcycle of the local bad boy. I felt positively giddy. And then the guilt hit. I loosened my grip a little and went back to looking at buildings and sights as we drove past.

I knew we were at the Grand Palace before he said anything. Grand is an understatement. Now this was a palace! I don't mean to take away from the other palaces I had seen, but this was regal.

The rest of the day was much the same. We went to Wat Prakeau and Wat Pho. I was absolutely blown away by my dream Thailand. Midafternoon we went to the Khao San Road Market and ate fruits and veggies and shopped. I picked out more gifts for the girls and Kendall paid for everything. I tried to refuse and went so far as to refuse to get things only to have him get them anyway and bring them to me.

Jill Edick

As the afternoon wore on he suggested we go back to my hotel so we could change for our dinner cruise. Cera was not back yet. I changed quickly, touched up my makeup and pulled my hair back in a clip although I wasn't sure how that would work with a helmet. I don't know why I even thought I would have to worry, when I went down to the lobby, Kendall was there in fresh clothes and the Mercedes was out front.

He opened the door for me then climbed in the other side. The driver took us to the pier where we got on our cruise with the Luxury Manohra Song. The boats were restored rice barges and were absolutely beyond my dreams.

Kendall held my hand as we boarded our boat. As the cruise began, we went past some of the magnificent sites we had visited just that day. The lights from the river were positively breathtaking. We were seated for dinner which was extravagant considering we were on a restored rice barge. Where could this wonderful food have come from? We couldn't have asked for better weather, food or an evening. It was simply put, magical. I was positively sad when it ended.

Like all good things though, it did end. Kendall took me back to the hotel and walked me up to my room. I could hear the tv on so I knew Cera was back. No doubt peeking out the peep hole watching.

"I can't thank you enough for the wonderful day Kendall. It was perfect, I had an amazing time."

"Me as well Lena. I cannot wait to see you in Chiang Mai. I will have to do some planning to make that part of your trip better than this night right now." Then he leaned in and kissed me. I was expecting it, which made it harder to push back the guilt. But the kiss was so deep and so soft that soon I was thinking about nothing but his lips on mine. I felt his hands on my hips and he pushed me up against the wall. The kissed deepened and I heard weird mewling noises, only to realize it was me. I didn't even remember where I was until Cera opened the room door and cleared her throat.

Truly

"Ahem, excuse me, didn't mean to interrupt. Also I don't want to spend the night soothing a guilty conscience."

She turned and went back in the room.

"I guess I was just asked to leave." Kendall smiled down at me. "I will see you in Chiang Mai soon. Until then Lena."

He walked away. He stopped and turned back to me. "You're not checking out my rear end again are you?" He winked and then left.

"Lena! Get your naughty self in here!"

So she had been watching. Well what did she expect, she was the one who told me to dress like bread.

What I walked into was not an angry Cera though. It was like old high school days. She was in her jammies in the middle of her bed. She threw my jammies at me and said to hurry up, she needed details!

I was laughing at her as I changed and joined her on the bed. She handed me a glass of wine. "You kissed, now TELL!"

I showed her pictures and told her all about my day.

"Wow. I am so jealous. How do I find Mr. Perfect?"

"Well, I guess you can have him, I am married after all. Shit! I did it again."

"You did nothing. You had fun. No guilt! I said it and I meant it, I am not soothing a guilty conscience. So get over it right now! Do you remember where the diner was? I think I would like to have breakfast there in the morning before that drive to Chiang Mai."

"I think I can find it."

"Perfect. Let's get some rest then. Have sexy sassy wonderful dreams Lena!"

I rolled my eyes at her. "Thanks Cera, and you as well!"

Chapter 11

Around the world:

"WHAT? HE DID WHAT?? THAT SON OF A BITCH!"

He started pacing around running his hands through his hair.

"I've already gone along with all of this for the damn money! Shit! This was OUR future, NOT that MOTHER FUCKERS!"

"I think we will get it back. It may just take longer now."

"LONGER? Like hell! What do you like fucking that piece of shit? HUH?? Like sucking his cock, taking it up your ass? HUH? YOU ARE MINE! I HAVE PUT UP WITH HIM FUCKING MY WOMAN AND BEATING MY WOMAN FOR LONG ENOUGH!"

"Don't talk that way. You know I hate him. I hate being his puppet. I was only doing this for us. For us." She is crying, embarrassed at the ugly truths she was hearing. Feeling like a worthless slut for doing what she had done.

"Look at me, LOOK at me. This isn't your fault. He's the pile of DOG SHIT! He is going to pay! I need you to do one more thing for me."

"What, anything, just please don't be mad at me."

"I'm not mad at you. I need to know what that fucker fears. Find out what he fears that I can use."

"That's easy." She smiles for the first time. "Rodents. He is terrified of rats."

Now he is smiling too. "Oh he will pay. HE WILL FUCKING PAY!"

Truly

Sexy, sassy and wonderful dreams I had indeed. They were so good and so bad. I woke with renewed guilt and pulled out my computer to send e-mails.

I sent the girls more pictures and they had sent me some too. It looked like they were having fun. There was a short message from Geoff. 'I cancelled the credit card because they couldn't fix their problems. Sorry.' Nothing else, not use another card, not do you have cash, I could wire you some money, nothing. Guilt be damned, now I was pissed off. I shot back a scathing message to that effect. I gave him the hotel in Chiang Mai we were going to be at and told him I had better have a wire there by tomorrow morning and in the meantime I was going to use another card. I told him that was terribly inconsiderate of him and if there were problems with the card he should have told me before I left. Doesn't he care that he sent me to another country with no money? I hit send before I could regret the things I wrote.

I got up and went to the bathroom, when I came back I was surprised to see a new message from Geoff. 'Use another card, money will be waiting.' Again that's it. No apologies, no love, no how is your trip, no have you heard from the girls. Nothing. I decided his rudeness could be met with some of my own. I did not reply with a thank you. My manners gene was screaming at me, but I ignored it. I bagged up the computer and got ready to leave.

I started a pot of coffee and was sitting down to read a book when Cera got up. "Was that you I heard beating up a computer keyboard this morning or was I dreaming?"

"No, that was me. I don't want to talk about it."

"OK, Sounds good to me. Give me an hour to get ready and packed up then we can go have breakfast. Do you think she will remember you enough to duplicate that breakfast you had yesterday?"

"I doubt it, why would she, but I know she speaks English well enough to understand what we want."

Jill Edick

Cera must have been hungry because 45 minutes later we were loading the car and driving to the diner.

I was surprised when we walked in, that Mama Xu remembered me. "Hello! Kenny girl come back! I so happy, come come, I have table for you with friend."

Cera whispered to me, "I think she remembers you."

We were led to a table that was already occupied. By Kendall.

"I thought I heard that terrible nickname being thrown about. Good morning ladies. Join me for some breakfast?"

"Well Kenny boy, I don't know about Lena, but I would be thrilled to have breakfast with you!" With that Cera sat down and looked to Mama Xu. "I would like what she had yesterday, it sounded marvelous!"

Mama Xu beamed and walked away.

Cera plopped down, literally plopped and took up the whole bench. I turned to Kendall. "Well Kenny, I guess I get to sit with you."

"Sunshine, you can sit wherever you want, but not if you ever call me Kenny again."

We all laughed and I crossed my heart. He scooted so I could sit next to him in the too tiny booth seat.

"Well Kenny, Lena promised, I didn't. Tell me all about yourself, leave out no details."

Cera was never one to be shy. But I think she met he match in Kendall.

"Well Cerapoo, in kindergarten I threw up on my teacher. In first grade I picked my nose and left it on the teacher's desk, in second grade I put a tarantula in my teacher's desk drawer, shall I continue?"

"Cerapoo? Is that the best you have?"

After another raucous round of laughter, I knew Kendall had won over Cera hook line and sinker. The conversation returned to more normal topics. Shortly thereafter we were served our breakfast. Today we were served sausage and eggs like yesterday, but we were given more traditional biscuits with it. The whole thing was fabulous indeed. I asked Kendal to get me that bread recipe, the pancake may not have been outstanding, but this woman could make biscuit bread things better than I ever would be able too. Once again, I was given a napkin of instruction in Thai, and Kendall took it with him for translation.

Kendall and Cera got into a bit of a wrestling match over the check and Mama Xu came over and scolded both for being babies and handed the check to me. I don't know when I got involved, but I guess I just did. I was still very confused about the baht's, so I handed a small pile of bills to Kendall with the check and told him to figure it out. He did. He threw out money from his pocket and handed me mine back and walked out the door before I could protest. Cera stormed past me growling about chauvinists and Mama gave me a hug and shooed me out the door behind the other two.

When I got outside they were chatting on the sidewalk and all seemed to be forgiven.

"I'll wait for you in the car Lena. See you later Kendall."

She walked away and Kendall wrapped me in a bear hug so quick I never saw it coming. Likewise, the kiss he then planted on me was such a surprise, just the way I like them from him, no time to think.

This time it was mama Xu who came out yelling at us. Apparently we were 'making customers sick with display'. But she smiled and I am pretty sure she gave Kendall a thumbs up.

He walked me to Cera's car where she was busy pretending to be reading a map. "I will see you soon Lena."

Then he closed the door and walked away.

"Wait, what? What did he mean see you soon? Cera?"

"Well you know he lives in Chiang Mai, and you have kept running into him here, so it doesn't seem to be that odd of a thought that you will probably run into him there."

"Oh, well I guess that makes sense."

"Can I ask you something Lena?"

"Of course." I was a little leery. She seemed more serious than normal.

"Well, I know how loyal you are. I know you would never ever cheat. I also know you are having a lot of guilt about everything Kendall. First, I don't think you should feel any guilt. Yes, kissing is walking that gray line of cheating, but in my opinion no biggie. Second, I don't want you to feel judged here, ok? But if you don't want the guilt, why are you allowing this to go so far? I swear, no guilt from me, I don't think you have done anything really wrong, other than hurting your own self opinion. But I am afraid you're going to be the one to get hurt here. If not now, later. I'm a little worried. You are getting serious and I don't want you hurt or disillusioned or to remember this trip with regrets."

It was like she had reached into my mind and was pulling out my concerns.

"Your absolutely right. I don't want any regrets. I don't want the guilt. I just don't understand these crazy feelings I'm having. I know much of it is probably just how angry I am at Geoff for his terrible behavior that I just don't understand. And Kendall is so kind and treated me like I have never been treated, even in the early days of my relationship with Geoff. But I am married and I need to make that very clear if I should run into Kendall again. I can't keep behaving like a school girl."

"What is going on with Geoff? I wasn't aware you had even spoken with him, did he finally get back to you about the credit card?"

"Yes, he finally responded. Well if that's what you call it." I told her about the e-mails and cancelled card, and that he never even asked about the girls and the girls said he hadn't called them or anything. "I just don't understand. He used to be at least an attentive dad even if he wasn't a perfect husband. And he never has been a bad husband, he has taken care of me. I've never had financial issues before and even in our early days, he took care of me. In recent years though it's like a switch flipped. I just don't understand. Is it work, is it me, is it parenthood? But even if he was feeling over being part of our family, why would he completely shut out his girls? They are his kids whether we are together or not. And why after all I gave up to help him gain the success would he cut me off completely? Why would he let me leave the country and shut off the credit card? I'm so confused."

"You should be. I'm confused too. I'm so sorry. I didn't realize things have been questionable for so long. Why haven't you told me? You know I'm always here for you."

"I know. But I wasn't and I'm still not sure that things are bad. I mean, could I just be making this up in my mind? I just don't know Cera. When did this all get so confusing?"

"Honey, I hate to say it, but have you thought maybe it's time for you to move on?"

"And go where Cera? I have no education, I dropped out when I got pregnant remember? I have no skills. I have no money to speak of. Don't get me started on my parents. Or have you forgotten, the lovely speech my drunk mother gave at the reception we had "you two made your bed, lie in it" remember that? I have three girls and no means with which to take care of them. But that is all mute. I love Geoff. I just don't understand where our lives went to askew. I asked him about a year ago if we could try some counseling. He freaked out at me."

"Well, I know you can't keep living this strange existence hon. Your obviously craving affection of the adult male kind. As well you should. Your young, beautiful and desirable. If Geoff is to damn blind to see it and refuses to get help to save your relationship, maybe you should remind him what spousal support and child support will cost him. Bastard cannot leave you girls destitute. If you want to save the marriage, but he is unwilling, maybe it's time to give up that ghost."

"I have thought about it. I just ... I'm just not ready yet. I know, I need to tell Kendall to leave me alone. I can't lead him on any longer. Your right, I am loving the affection and attention. But I'm not available to return it. If I see him again I will tell him. I don't want to think about Geoff anymore though. I want to enjoy this trip. I've got just two weeks left and I want to enjoy this time. I know I need to think about life after, but I would rather put it off. Just for now."

"OK, for now. I want you to have fun. So on that note, I made you a list. I know how you love my famous lists. But I thought you might like to book a few excursions when we get to the hotel. I have a suite of rooms there, so please feel free to come and go as you want. I wish I could spend more time with you up here, but I only have two weeks to get a ton of stuff done."

"It's ok Cera. I will be just fine. I am looking forward to some activities. Thank you for the list. I'm so excited. I can't wait to see the rooms. Maybe I will even find a market and get some great food and make you dinner some evening."

"Ha, well you know I would like that! But don't feel like you have to do that. We have room service and restaurants at the hotel. Eat what you want and charge it to the room. After my work pays my part of the bill, I'll let you know if there is any balance I can't handle. We will figure it out. Just enjoy and don't worry about money ok?"

"Thank you Cera. I promise, I will live it up. There better be a wire waiting for me in the morning though."

"Well if there is or isn't, don't worry. Remind me to give you a lesson in Thai money tonight too so you aren't out there buying a $2 item for $20 because you don't understand the currency"

"That bad huh?"

We passed the rest of the drive looking at Rice Paddy's and the workers in them in silence.

Truly

I must have dozed off. The next thing I saw was the outskirts of a village.

"Oh my, Cera, I'm so sorry. I did not mean to fall asleep."

"It's ok, how could you not with the oh so exciting scenery. But it is getting better. I think we are getting closer. We are getting into a more mountainous region."

"Oh good. I'm done with this car. So what sights do you think I should see?"

We spent the rest of the car ride discussing sights she thought I should see. I decided that I was going to join Cera at the pool this afternoon and for a nice dinner, then early night. I was really fascinated about a tea plantation tour and definitely another market. I was going to talk to concierge to see what they had to offer.

We were definitely arriving in a larger town, but certainly not a city. It was so beautiful though. You could see temples on the horizon and the mountains in the back ground. It was a beautiful town. I couldn't wait to go out exploring. We pulled up to a beautiful resort. It took my breath away.

"Oh Cera, this is amazing! We are spending at least two full weeks here?"

"Yup. We'll see how long my job takes, maybe a bit longer. It is pretty nice. Best digs my work has paid for. If they keep this up, you're coming with me every trip I take. I usually get some dump ass place with an iffy at best pool. This looks like it might have a pool I'll actually get into. Come on, lets get checked in."

We got settled it our suite and changed to go to the pool. We had a fun afternoon and evening. I was ready for bed. I sent a few emails to the girls and crashed out.

Chapter 12

I got up with Cera in the morning and went to the concierge to check out tours. I found one I wanted to take but it didn't leave for another 3 hours. The concierge desk suggested I go walk along one of the morning markets that were close by. So I went to a close by market and was waiting to cross a street when I saw him.

He had on a different prosthesis, it looked like a hook on the end of his leg. Like one you saw runners use. He had no shirt on and was sweating and glistening in the sun. My breath caught in my throat. He was magnificent. The sunlight caught the red in his hair and he was looking on fire! I decided I needed to get away before I went into school girl mode again. So I quickly turned back towards to hotel and started walking as fast as I could. It was not fast enough however. A few seconds later he ran up next to me.

"You ought to know by now I can feel your stare on my ass. Why did you run away? Do you not like sweat?"

"Oh, no, that's not a problem. You look… umm..So, you're a runner? That's interesting."

I could not even believe I just said that. I was going back to the hotel and drowning myself. What the hell was wrong with me?

He didn't seem to mind my momentary moronic behavior, he just laughed.

"Do you have anything planned for your day?"

"Oh, yes, I am going on a tour of a tea plantation. I was just taking a walk to pass time until the tour leaves."

Truly

"That sounds fun, kind of. Well, it's not my cup of tea actually, pun intended."

That was so terrible and I started laughing so hard I almost choked.

"Chock up a point for the guy! I'm going to go finish my run and then I have a meeting with my step father to discuss my trip. I would like to see you though. Can I call on you at your hotel later?"

"Sure, that would be great. Maybe you can advise me on some other things I can do while we are in the area. I'm a little nervous getting out on my own, so if you can suggest some American friendly activities that would be great."

"I would be happy to advise you dear Lena. On anything you need to know about. Until later."

He turned and took off running. It was an amazing sight to watch. I couldn't run and I had two legs. As I stood there watching, he reached behind himself and pointed at his butt then gave me a thumbs up. I was definitely drowning myself!

I got back to the hotel and I still had over two hours before my tour left and I had accomplished nothing with my morning other than making an ass of myself. I was contemplating drinking early but decided to stroll through the gardens at the resort instead. It was a picture perfect day, even the temperatures and humidity weren't completely intolerable. I took dozens of pictures of the flowers all around the resort. I found a beautiful walkway with handrails shaped and painted like dragons. I didn't realize how fast the time had gone by until I looked at my watch and had to hurry to make my tour on time.

The tour itself was fun and interesting. Contrary to Kendall's belief, I found tea to be most interesting. The plantation was beautiful and learning about how the tea is picked and processed and which parts of the leaves were used for different types of tea was fascinating. I never realized how much science there was to tea but I really enjoyed learning about it. So of course I had to buy a bunch of teas, a new beautiful tea pot, tea strainers and two books.

When I got back to the resort Cera was not back yet. There was a message for me from her saying she would not be back for dinner. So I cleaned up a bit and went down to one of the dining areas. I was just walking in and I saw Kendall. He waved and came over.

"Ready for some dinner?"

"Yes, I was just coming down for some, care to join me?"

"I would rather take you out. There is a night bazaar with lots of food stuff and parades. I thought I could take you there."

"Sounds fun. Let me just go put on some better walking shoes."

It was still light out when we arrived, so we walked around and shopped and sampled foods. It was quite good. As it started to get darker, the colorful lights went on and parades started walking through the market. There was music and dancing and the big dragons snaking their way around. It was truly a beautiful event. I was running out of words to describe all the amazing things I was seeing.

We finally headed back to the hotel.

"Would you like to take a walk through the gardens Lena? I believe I was going to offer up some ideas for your tourist eye. It's such a lovely night and the stars are out. Let's walk and I'll share some thoughts."

He had actually given me a list of places and was telling me about them. I was excited to see if there were any tours through the hotel for some of them. We walked for a while until we came to a grassy area.

"Let's stop here and look at the stars."

"Look at the stars, I love doing that, but rarely do I get to do it."

"That is a shame dear Lena. It is sad that as adults we often forget to just stop and enjoy the miracles around us."

"Your right. I guess I hadn't thought about it."

"Doesn't surprise me. It's not you personally, but many people forget what it is to enjoy life, be grateful for the little things and remember to stop and smell the roses. Americans especially. I found that when I was in the US. Everyone was in such a hurry and angry at anyone and everyone for anything and nothing. The big cities you can't even enjoy a night view of the sky. It made me very sad. Life is to short to not appreciate even the smallest of things."

He was right. Every day was about hurrying up to get ready and go, most likely to someplace you don't want to go to. Then spending hours not enjoying a minute before hurrying home to do chores and crashing exhausted into bed. Only to not get enough sleep before getting up to do it all again. I wished my time away until Geoff came home to see us. But then we spent almost no time together enjoying each other, but rather arguing about meaningless things like cars.

I was lost in these thoughts staring up at the stars.

"I wonder, if I'm here and you go home, if we both look up at the night sky, will we be looking at the same stars?"

"Well, that is deep. I don't know. Probably not, we are on different times, it wouldn't be possible really."

"Well obviously not literally, but suppose we set a day and time each week. And at our respective times, we went out and looked up. Would we see the same things? I think that would be awesome. To know somewhere in this world someone was thinking of me and sharing the same thing I had experienced or I was experiencing something they already had. It's not meant to be literal, but one of those slow down and remember the good things, the important things, the things that give us peace."

I didn't really know how to respond. The sentiment was beautiful, the idea heartwarming.

"I know your married Lena. I know you're going home to him. But I also know I have never met anyone like you. I believe there is that one special person we are meant to be with. We may make a few detours on our life path finding that someone. But ultimately you do find them. I would never ask you to leave your family for me. But I will ask that you remember me. I will always remember you. And when the time is right, I believe we will be together. If not this life, then the next. But for the time we have here and now, I want to share as many moments as I can with you. When you leave, I vow right now, every Thursday night, at 10:00 pm, I am going to lay in my yard and look at the stars and think of you. Every Thursday for the rest of my life."

I didn't realize I had tears streaming down my face until he leaned over me and started to kiss them away. I knew right then, I would never forget him and I too would be out looking at the stars with him, every Thursday forever.

We lay there for a while longer holding each other's hands talking quietly. He pointed out constellations and told me the stories he knew about them.

Eventually Kendall walked me up to my room.

"I don't want to make you uncomfortable Lena. I know I have been forward with you and I feel bad if I have made you uncomfortable."

"Kendall, please don't feel bad. I have been an active participant and I regret nothing."

He smiled at me and leaned in for a kiss. Unlike our previous kisses, this was soft and gentle. It sent shivers all down my spine. Then it was over. I felt intoxicated. That was the single most romantic kiss I had ever experienced. I decided right then that I would not have any guilt over anything for the rest of my time here in Thailand. Life is indeed too short for unimportant hang ups, and guilt was one of those.

Chapter 13

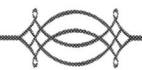

Kendall and I spent the next week together. He took me to so many different places. We went to the national park and an elephant sanctuary. We went to temples and palaces and gardens. We even went to a zoo. We had dinner in different places every night and when he brought me back to the hotel, we would walk to our spot in the garden and look up at the stars and talk.

I would return to my room at night and tell Cera about my day. She always seemed so excited to hear about it. She never seemed to judge me or act mad at me. It was refreshing to be able to share these happy moments with someone who wanted to share them with me and didn't make me feel bad.

"Oh Lena, I can't remember ever seeing you so animated and happy! I'm so happy for you. I hope you don't come down to hard when you go home. I can't imagine having the time you are having and then walking away from it."

"Me neither Cera. How am I going to do it? I know I should just start distancing myself now, but I can't. I just can't."

"I know, I know. I will help you through it. For now, enjoy this. You are so lucky."

I spent any free moments I had sending pictures to the girls and looking at pictures they sent me. It looked like I wasn't the only one having the time of my life. The girls were all getting so tanned and had so many tales to tell me. Even Lindy the queen of teen hormones was sending me pictures and long stories. She was just sure her and Marc were 'in love'. She even asked if we could move to Colorado one night when we were skyping.

Jill Edick

None of us though, had heard another word from Geoff. Not a word. No e-mails, text messages, nothing. To be fair, I stopped e-mailing him too. The 2nd card I brought with me was working and as promised, there had been money waiting for me when we checked into the hotel. So I really didn't feel anything else needed to be said. He hadn't responded to any of my earlier messages and pictures, so he must not be interested right?

The next day Kendall arrived on his motorcycle to take me to some less touristy parts of the mountains. He said he was taking me to one of his favorite hikes in this area and for a picnic he made himself.

It was a glorious day. He absolutely knew the best places to go. It was private and peaceful. Even the lunch was good. I didn't believe him that he made it. After much badgering her finally admitted his mother had made the lunch for us.

"Oy, a momma's boy. You still make your mom pack your lunch?"

"No, I didn't make her. I think she wants to see me married to a nice girl and if her packing for me makes your heart swoon then that is what she will do."

I laughed quite a bit about that. "So you haven't told her your courting a married woman then huh?"

"And ruin all this homemade food opportunity I've been given? No way!"

As we were headed back from our hike Kendall laid a bomb on me.

"So next week, I need to do some work around our farms for my father. I thought maybe you would like to join me for a few days. See my home and how things work in Thailand compared to America. My mom finished translating the recipes and has offered to teach you those as well as some other traditional Thai recipes if you're interested."

"That would be fun, but I hate to impose on your home. I can stay at the hotel; I don't want to be a burden."

Truly

"First, you are never a burden, Second, my home is not that close to the hotel. You would actually be doing me a favor by not having to drive here every night for our stargazing. I have been staying in town at my apartment this past week, but I really need to get back to the ranch for a while. That said, I will see you every night and I don't care if I have to drive two hours to do it. You coming home with me for a few days would be great for me. And NOT an imposition. Listen, talk it over with Cera, let me know in the morning. I will come by here and have breakfast with you and you can let me know your decision then. Fair?"

"Fair. Thank you for the invite. I think it would be fun to meet your family and definitely learn some skills in the kitchen."

That night I told Cera what Kendall had proposed. She didn't really say much. She seemed to be contemplating something. Then she picked up her phone and called someone, I am guessing her boss. She told them she would not be in until mid-morning, she had something she needed to do in the morning and hung up on whoever it was.

"OK, that taken care of, I will join you both for breakfast in the morning. I don't like the idea of you running off without knowing where you're going for 'days'. And don't look at me that way. I am not your mother, but that doesn't mean I can't worry about some unknown escapade your about to embark on."

"OK mom, I mean Cera. Geesh! Seriously, I'm glad you're here to grill him, as much as I want to go with him, I too am a little leery about just disappearing."

"I know what you mean, it's those one legged, nice ass hunks that are always the serial killers. The good ones are taken, gay or should be in jail. That is why I'm still single. I might add happily!"

We both laughed and drank a bottle of wine and laughed some more. Finally, we turned in for bed.

Chapter 14

Across the World:

"I'm so sorry. Please forgive me. I can fix it. I can. Please don't leave me. I need you."

"Of course I forgive you. I know you'll get it back. We will get through this together."

They stood there holding on to each other for a few minutes.

"Listen, I want to do something for you. You have had a rough time. Let me do something special for you. Let's go get some dinner, my treat. I know, lets' go to that super cute café uptown that I love so much!"

"Anything for you beautiful!"

"Let's walk, the weather has been lovely. Let's stroll hand in hand together."

"When did you become such a romantic? Of course, I would love to walk with you."

"How does tomorrow night sound?"

We were not looking real great when we got up in the morning.

"Damn Lena, your turning me into a cheap date. I never used to get drunk so easily. Where's the damn Tylenol?"

We each went to our bathrooms and started to get ready for breakfast. I was just getting out of the shower and pulled on a robe when I heard a knock at the door. Cera's shower was still running so I looked to see who was there. It was Kendall. Either he was early or I was late. I opened the door completely forgetting I was not really presentable yet.

"Wow! When I said I would take you for breakfast, I didn't mean you were the breakfast. Not that I'm complaining!"

Just like that I was pulled into his arms and had his lips pressed against mine. He had me in the room and the door kicked closed without so much a moving a hand from my waist. He deepened the kiss as he backed me up to the sofa in our room and we both tumbled down onto it. I felt my robe come loose and his hand was covering my breast while his lips worked their way down my neck. I was lost in another world.

"Well excuse me, pardon me, perhaps I should come back to my own room later?"

Whoa shit. I really had forgotten everything. Kendall was on his feet and I was pulling my robe closed. Cera was standing there before us with her toothbrush in hand and giving us the most impressive imitation of my mother I had seen since I last saw my mother. I couldn't help it, I burst out laughing.

"Exactly what is so funny young lady?" Cera screeched just like my mother while shaking her toothpaste covered toothbrush. I thought I was going to roll off the couch I was laughing so hard.

Kendall looked totally confused. Especially when Cera fell on the sofa with me and we were both laughing. We both had tears rolling down our eyes and I started hiccupping before he finally found his words.

"What the bloody hell is this all about? Why do I feel like I just walked into a private circus?"

"You did! Ha! When we were teens Lena's mom caught me in their basement with my boyfriend at the time. Lena was still asleep and her mom flipped her lid. She was yelling at me and the boy and pointing her toothbrush at us. She was so worked up there was toothpaste flying everywhere. Lena came out to see what was going on and her mom threw the toothbrush and hit her in the forehead with it. The boy, I don't even remember his name, ran for it. It was hysterical."

"Oh well, I certainly understand the humor...not really but if you promise to not tag me with your toothbrush I will pretend."

"Promise. Well that was fun kids. I think I will finish getting ready for breakfast. Lena, may I suggest you dress before opening the door in the future?"

Cera turned and went back to her room. I stood and excused myself to get dress and dry my hair, and mostly regather my thoughts. Between the moment with Kendall and the moments with Cera, I was pretty well in need of a nap I think, definitely I needed that Tylenol mentioned earlier.

When I returned to the sitting room a bit later Cera was there and her and Kendall were chatting.

"Cera tells me she is joining us for breakfast with the intent of grilling me until I gave up all my secrets. Should be a fun meal."

"Cera! Oh my goodness!"

"What, I'm not letting my best friend just disappear into the wilds of Thailand without knowing if the one taking her away is a serial killer or not. He will be grilled and he will like it. Period, end of story. Now are two ready, I'm starving and have a bitch of a headache."

Cera confidently strode out of the room while Kendall and I watched after her.

"Wow, remind me not to admit to being a serial killer at breakfast would you?"

I just laughed at him and we followed after Cera.

Grill him she did, she even asked if he was a serial killer. I almost spewed my coffee across the table when she did that. But by the end of breakfast, she had address phone numbers and family names and a pretty detailed itinerary for me. He only intended to keep me for about three days then bring me back to finish being a tourist before the end of the trip. And he did admit to being a serial killer in a past life, but he was pretty sure he didn't have those urges in this life. Cera threw some sort of a berry at him. Unfortunately, he ducked and it pegged someone else in the back of the head.

And so the circus continued. Cera and I left Kendall to apologize and make nice while we tried not to laugh until we made it to our room. We were unsuccessful.

Chapter 15

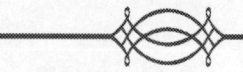

Cera helped me pack a small bag to take with me all the while lecturing me on the importance of protection.

"Hold that thought for a minute, I'll be right back."

She darted out of the room and came back in a few minutes later with a box of condoms and a pistol.

"What the hell Cera? Where did you get that?"

"The drug store, really, not difficult, but I wasn't sure if Adonis out there would bother."

"Not the condoms, the gun!"

"Oh, my company always provides me with one while I'm in the field. I pick it up when I report in that way I don't have to deal with the hassle of traveling with a gun."

"But why? What do you need a gun for? And if you need a gun, why would you give that to me?"

"Well, I sometimes get into some not to great places with not the friendliest sorts of people. I've never had to use the gun, but it has been nice to have. I don't think I will need it here, plus I have an assistant this trip because of the speed they are wanting things done. So we will have another gun with us. You take it and blow his balls off if you need to. You remember how to shoot right?"

"Yes, I remember how to shoot. I still practice once in a while. I really hope I won't need it, but thanks."

"Not a problem. You owe me though. You are going into an interesting part of the country, bring back some local wine ok?"

"Ha! We are turning into complete lushes on this trip."

"Turning? Just this trip? Really? I need to get to work. Have fun, but be safe ok?"

"I will. Thank you Cera. Again. For everything!"

We hugged and then she left for work. I gathered my bag and went out to find Kendall sitting on the couch reading a newspaper.

When he saw me he stood. "Are you ready to go? I can't wait to show you my home."

"Well let's go then. I'm excited for another adventure."

As we walked out, he suddenly stopped and turned to me.

"Lena, I'm sorry for what happened this morning. I was entirely out of line. You have my word it won't happen again."

"Thank you Kendall. If I recall though I wasn't protesting. So let's just say we should both keep more clothes on and we will be perfectly well behaved."

He started chuckling. "Well, I will keep that in mind too, but when I run, I rarely wear a shirt and always wear running shorts. Will you be able to keep your hands to yourself?"

"It will be hard, but as long as I can watch, I think I will be able to keep my hands occupied."

We had arrived at the exit of the hotel. The Mercedes was there waiting for us.

He was right about the drive. It was a solid two hours until we got to his ranch. Ranch was really not the right word. Sprawling mini city was more accurate. There was a huge house front and center as we drove up a long drive. Off to one side was a smaller house, but still very beautiful. There was a separate building for a garage. And further down the drive you could see what looked like apartments in the distance.

"This is the main house. My parents live in the big house. I built and took over the smaller one when I turned 21. Down the road we have apartments for the workers and their families. We also have a small store and gas station that get stocked weekly. We also have a small community center for the families including a pool. Because we are so far from everything, we also offer a shuttle for the children when school is in session. It takes them into town for school and back in the evenings so the families don't have to worry."

"Wow. It's like its own town."

"Well it kind of is. We have several hundred employees. We have another apartment community at the other end of the ranch. Because of the huge nature of the businesses and the multifaceted nature of the businesses, we need to keep people close. We found it's cheaper and easier, not to mention improves employee loyalty if we offer these things. It's much more efficient. We also have a security unit. Their apartments are in yet another area of the ranch. They help keep the peace and protect the property. At that area we also have administrative offices where the paper pushing happens. That's a huge operation in and of itself. There is a small apartment area for them as well. Nowhere near this size. Administration is a nightmare, but can be handled with much smaller numbers of people."

"How big is this ranch? It must be huge!"

"Well the buffalo operation alone encompasses the equivalent of about 50 of your football fields not including the buildings. That is just the pasture land. The poultry division encompasses about 20 football fields not including buildings. Between both operations we have about 20 assorted buildings for processing animals and feed and veterinary care. We also have a huge shipment area where we keep trucks for various uses and mechanic buildings. And there is also the power and water buildings we have. We use well water as much as possible, but we also have an extensive irrigation system as well as treatment plants

Truly

for the people who live here. Also, there is a rain collection system in place. We have a solar power field and a wind farm. We have pretty sophisticated green systems in place. That was part of what I took over after college. I wanted to find a way to be more ecofriendly. My step dad has always been a leader in organic farming. All the poultry are free range. They do not live in cramped feeding barns. Even the egg sheds are animal friendly. The buffalo are free range and organically fed. We have some of the healthiest live stock in Thailand. We only buy new livestock from suppliers that meet the same care requirements that we adhere to. This is a huge operation. I will give you a tour of it all later."

"This is amazing! Where do you have the rice paddies? Are those here too?"

"No, the rice paddies are more to the south and west. You probably drove past many of them on your way up to Chiang Mai from Bangkok. At one point we owned most of that land. My dad has sold at least half of the rice operation and leased out another 25% to other farmers. We only maintain about 25% of the business now. Because that area is closer to villages, we don't have the same set up as we do here. The employees come to work, do their jobs, and then go to their own homes at the end of the day. However even those operations are controlled by the administrators here."

"This is overwhelming. How much of the operations do you take care of?"

"I am in charge of implementing new ecofriendly systems and researching ways to keep the farms running clean and the animals living organically. That said, I have my own group of employees that handle the day to day of that. I also work with our quality control group. That allows me to travel, which I love. I also assist in the purchasing of new livestock when it is time to rotate stock to help prevent crossbreeding and disease. My step dad and I travel a lot every couple years to visit farms and purchase new breeding stock. I guess you can say I'm a jack of many trades. I try to stay away from the ranch though. I believe I can do more by being out there looking for new ideas and working with clients. That is what I enjoy."

"I am seriously impressed. This is, simply put, an amazing operation."

"Thank you. I never fancied myself a farmer, but I have found there is a lot more to farming that riding around in tractors wearing overalls."

"Well I guess I wouldn't mind seeing you doing that, but I can understand your desire not to."

We both laughed at that thought.

"KENDALL MORGAN! GET YOURSELF UP TO THIS HOUSE AND HUG YOUR MOTHER RIGHT NOW!"

"Oops. We better get to the house before my mom has a total fit. Prepare yourself, I'm about to get lectured on my rude behavior and neglecting my mother and failing to introduce you. Wait for it...."

We walked up to the house. His mom was standing on the porch. She was absolutely beautiful. Wow. I know where Kendall gets his looks. Unlike his blonde hair with red highlights, hers was the color of fire. She had to be at least 5'10 and very curvy. She was stunning. She also looked like a ticked off mom.

"What is the meaning Kenny! You bring a guest home and stand outside for thirty minutes without even inviting her in and introducing her. What rudeness is this? I taught you better. Now you apologize to us both immediately then introduce us!"

"I'm sorry mama. Lena, I apologize. I should have invited you in and allowed you the chance to freshen up after the drive. Please forgive my poor hospitality. Mama, this is Lena, Lena this is my mom Shanna."

"That's better. Now I suggest you mind yourself young man. You may be 34, but I'm still your mom and you will have respect. I did not raise a heathen." Then she turned to me, I admit, I was terrified. "Lena darling, welcome to our ranch. I imagine Kenny was just boring you to tears about the place. I swear the men around here are just in love with dirt and critters and can't get enough yapping about them. Come on in dear, I will show you to your rooms." Then she turned and walked into the house.

"Kenny, bring Lena's bags, don't just stand there!"

"You better follow, I'll come rescue you in a few." Then he turned and left to get my bag.

Well this was not how I was expecting the week to start. I followed Shanna into the house. Wow. It was like being in America. I would never have guessed I was in Thailand. "This is just beautiful ma'am. It feels like I'm back home."

"Why thank you. I was raised in Australia. I traveled to America for school. I went on a trip to Alaska with some friends my senior year and that is where I met Kenny's father. Well, you see how that turned out. I finished school and came back to Australia after he denied Kendall. But that is ok. I met a wonderful man and he gave me the freedom to do what I wanted with our home. I modeled it after Australian, British and American décor. I find it fun and eclectic. Most of our friends find it tacky. But I think they are just jealous."

We both laughed. I could see how someone might call this tacky, but I loved it. Shanna took me down a hall and showed me to a room.

"This is our guest wing. You have a dressing sitting room, a bedroom and a private bath. Please make yourself comfortable. Out that window over there you can see Kenny's house. I will let you clean up from your drive. Kenny should be here soon with your bags and he can show you around the houses. I will have lunch set out in the kitchen shortly."

I was exploring the rooms when Kendall came in.

"Well hey there Kenny."

"Uhg! I hate that name! Please never let it leave your lips again."

"Well I will make you a deal, never call me Dar I will never call you Kenny. Fair?"

"Perfect! Shall we shake on it?"

We did.

"So, my mother informs me that I am in charge of giving you a tour of the houses, then I'm to have you back in 30 minutes for lunch. I was also told that she would be giving you cooking lessons after lunch while I tended to my business. Unless of course you need a nap after the drive. I don't know why drives seem to stress my mother so, she thinks everyone needs a shower and a nap after two hours in the car. Anyway, if you are up to it, that is her plan for the day. Feel free to tell her to go away."

"I think cooking sounds fun! I can't wait to see the rest of this house and yours. Be nice to your mom, she is just being a good hostess. And I will not tell her to go away. I like her!"

"I like her too, but hold off on judgment until you see the rest of the house. I will let you change your mind."

We both laughed. He started the tour with the rest of the guest wing. I was apparently in the American room. There was also as promised, a British room and Australian room. She did like her themes. The rest of the house was much the same way. Lots of bric a brac and odds and ends, but everything just fit. It worked. I made a mental note to send her some décor items from Colorado when I go there to pick up the girls.

"So, are you ready for the man cave? No themes over here besides comfort."

"Oh, man cave? I hope it doesn't smell." I winked at him.

"Just like me." He winked back.

Everything here was quite neutral. Shades of brown and tan everywhere, It was actually very comfortable and nice looking. The furniture was all overstuffed and super soft looking. You just wanted to jump on it. I could picture myself here curled up on the squishy couch with a book and a blanket. It was a nice space for a bachelor. Not too big, nothing fancy, everything you need, nothing you don't. It was perfect.

"Well what do you think of the houses?"

"I love them! I get the feeling your step dad must be content to not have his own space, because if he has one, I haven't seen it."

"Oh he does, his office. He left the house to mom. When I built this place I banned mom from it and hired a real decorator."

"I bet your mom was pissed!"

"That is an understatement. She won't come over here other than to knock on the door and tell me whatever it is she needs. Wont set foot inside. Dad will though. He likes it here. It's a bit of an argument. I stay out of it. I figure I built this place I'm going to have it how I want it just like she did. She seemed to respect that argument, because she doesn't say much about it anymore. If I were you though, I would tell her you hate it if she asks."

"I will not lie. I like both houses. They are both very personal and that is what makes them perfect."

"That is what make you perfect. You see the beauty in everything. Thank you Lena." He pulled me into a hug, that's all, just a wonderful tight hug. I loved it.

"I better get you over to the kitchen before mom has both our hides."

He grabbed my hand and we left his house. As we were walking to the main house I asked him why I wasn't staying in his house.

"Are you nuts? My mom would not have that. First, you are married, second not to me. That would be highly unethical. I may be a product of a one-night stand, but she will not have any virtue busting activities going on under her roof. You are a guest, you will stay in a guest room and no names will be tarnished."

Jill Edick

I burst out laughing. Surely he was kidding. But the look he gave me said he wasn't.

"I'm sorry for laughing, obviously this is serious business here. My apologies."

"Don't sweat it. My mom isn't that big of a prude, but she likes her appearances. I think it was because she caught a lot of hell when she came home pregnant with me. Her parents were furious. She was not allowed back in their house. She had to get a job and support us on her own. Then she married an, gasp, Asian. My gosh. The shame. My grandparents are from another planet I think. The only thing they approve of with this marriage is he's rich. We don't see my grandparents. But now my mom has taken to hiding anything she feels may cause embarrassment. It's easier to hide it than stand up for it I guess."

"How sad for her, her own parents condemning her instead of helping. That make me sad. How sad you don't get to know your grandparents either. That is more of a loss in my opinion than a bit of momentary embarrassment over situations life deals you. What is really sad is the cards you were dealt weren't bad. You're a wonderful person, and though I don't know your step dad, he has obviously provided for you and your mother. Why didn't they have more children?"

"Well, my mom had a hard delivery with me. Not great health care because she had no insurance and her parents wouldn't help her. So I was born and we both survived, but it wasn't pretty. She was told there would be no more kids and though I think they tried, it never did happen. They considered adoption. But there are so many kids around this place, you'll see tomorrow, and my mom loves organizing big events for them. There are huge monthly birthdays, and holiday parties. There is always an event for the kids around here. They eventually decided not having any of their own was ok. They have a blast with everyone else's."

"And how about you Kendall, do you want kids?"

"Yes and no. I love kids, but I don't feel like I have to have my own to be complete. I feel like I'm at the age that any lady I fall in love with will be a similar age and kids may not be an option. Or there may already be

Truly

kids. I'm ok with that. I learned well from my mom. I don't need blood brothers and sisters, I have hundreds right around here. This is family. I'm happy in that knowledge."

"That is really nice. It's actually very refreshing. I have so many 'friends' that have stipulations for relationships, like children, houses, hell even my husband thinks our relationship makes or breaks because of a stupid car. You just want to love someone. The rest will work itself out. There is a very lucky lady in your future. I think I'm jealous."

"Are you two going to stand out here all day while the lunch I made wastes away, or would you like to eat and then I can have my student for the afternoon? I have a fabulous dinner menu lined up, I need Lena!"

"Sorry mom. Of course I'm going to eat lunch, I'm sure Lena won't say no to that. But go easy on her mom, geesh. She's supposed to be a guest not a chef."

"Thanks Kendall, but I'm excited. I would love to help you make dinner tonight. I hope I don't disappoint."

We had a small but delicious lunch. Then Shanna sent Kendall packing so she could start teaching her 'student'. I had a super time. I learned so much. Shanna was a great teacher and so much fun. She had stories to go with every recipe and whose favorite this was and what went best with that. She even made me a little cookbook that included the two recipes from the little diner in Bangkok. I was so honored. Shanna was a great cook. We were having so much fun, I didn't even realize how late it had gotten until Kendall and a man I had not met walked in.

"Mom, Lena, good evening! Lena this is my step father, you can call him Jim, everyone does."

"Jim, good to meet you. Thank you for inviting me into your home. It is lovely. I hope you like the dinner I have helped with."

"Ms. Lena. Lovely name. I am sure we will enjoy the meal. Shanna is a great cook, if you were in the kitchen with her all afternoon and she didn't throw you out, I'm sure it will be outstanding. Shanna my love.

You look lovely this evening. When shall we convene to the dining room?"

"Give us ten minutes handsome."

I helped Shanna move huge amounts of food to the dining room where the guys had already sat. Jim said a traditional Thai blessing and then it was a free for all. I felt right at home. I couldn't help think the girls would have loved this. A couple of the more traditional dishes I didn't care much for. Ironically those were the one's Jim loved the best.

We had a great time chatting and eating. Finally, Jim excused himself. He had some work to finish up before meetings tomorrow. Kendall and I helped Shanna clean up.

"If it's alright with you ladies, I would like to steal Lena and show her the stars for a while."

He held his hand to me and we started to leave, but not before I saw the look on Shanna's face. She didn't look angry, but certainly worried.

"I have meetings until lunch tomorrow. After that can I interest you in a tour of the ranch?"

"I think that would be fun. Thank you Kendall."

"I was also thinking that tomorrow night I could interest you in dinner and dancing?"

"Dinner and dancing? Where on earth would we do that out here?"

"Well, let me work out those details. You don't worry about a thing. The next day I have meetings in the morning and early afternoon. I think we should be able to go back to Chiang Mai in the evening though. I can show you my apartment there if you like, or return you to the hotel."

"So soon? We just got here, are you really going to be ready to return?"

"Yup. I do a lot of things via computer, so my stuff here is just touching base, signing things, nothing major. Just loose ends that need to be tied up periodically."

We had just reached the far side of his house. You couldn't see the main house from here. On the ground was a huge blanket for us to lie on as well as a bottle of that awesome pineapple wine I liked so much.

We lay on the blanket and talked while he pointed out the constellations again for me. We enjoyed the wine. It was a perfect end to a fun day.

Finally, he walked me back to the main house and my rooms. He did not give me a kiss, but rubbed my arms and winked then walked away. I missed the kiss, but I loved watching him walk away.

Chapter 16

Across the world:

They were walking hand in hand, no other people around. They walked past a dark ally, not really paying attention.

Suddenly he was grabbed from behind and a stun gun was at his neck and volts of electricity shot into him and he collapsed.

He felt himself being dragged into the dark ally.

His assailant stood over him. "What are you thinking now? HUH?"

He was slapped across the face.

Where was she at? What happened to her? He hoped she ran for help.

But then there she was. Standing next to the guy.

"Surprise you bastard! May I introduce you? This is my husband! I think he has a few things to say to you about fucking his wife then fucking our retirement over."

He felt another jolt from the stun gun. This time his bowels loosened.

"Oh looky, the filthy pig shit himself!"

"You disgust me scumbag! I think it's time to Die you mother fucker! Did you really think your better than everyone? You're a cheater a liar and a no good fucking thief! Die you stupid bastard. Hell is too good for you!"

He tried to scream but couldn't feel his face from the stunning. It didn't matter because the first blow came to his throat where the man stabbed him in the vocal cords, severing them completely.

Then they were both over him with what looked like ice picks.

"Ladies first, anything in particular you want to take a bit of revenge on love?"

"Oh yeah! Did I ever tell you how bad you were in bed? You suck!" Then the shank in her hand came down in his privates.

He was trying to scream again but couldn't. He was stunned again. The pain was intense and terrible. He couldn't move, he couldn't speak. For the first time he believed he was about to die.

The couple started shanking him, taking turns stabbing him again and again in his stomach and lower. It felt like they stabbed him for hours, but it was surely only seconds. Then it stopped.

She stood over him again. "You think we are done? Oh we have only just begun you bastard!"

She was covered in his blood, dripping over him. He felt sick.

Then the guy was back holding a bag.

"So mother fucker, what do you fear? I have a special bag of hell here for you. I hope you're not afraid of RATS!"

Then he opened the bad and turned it on him. Rats fell out all over him. He was trying to move away, trying to scream. Nothing worked. The rats started licking at the blood and picking at his flesh. He was horrified and begging for death. When would it end.

The couple stood there laughing forever. They seemed to be enjoying the show. If he could speak he would have begged for death. The rats eating him was the final blow.

The man walked over to him. "See you in hell!" His leg went back and he never saw another thing.

Chapter 17

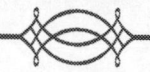

I slept really well, although I was having some seriously weird dreams. But I actually slept later than I normally would. When I got up I spent some time skyping with the girls. After that I took a nice leisurely bath. I loved baths, but hadn't had the opportunity to take one on this trip. It felt so nice to sink into the water for an hour. I totally lost track of time and soon I heard a knock at the door and Kendall saying lunch was ready. I hadn't even had breakfast. I found that thought didn't even bother me I had been enjoying my morning so much.

I quickly got dressed and joined Kendall and Shanna for lunch. Once again it was outstanding. The woman could cook! I couldn't wait to start making some of her recipes for my family.

After lunch Kendall took me on a tour of the ranch. He had a cart waiting out front for us to ride in, he said there was no way we were walking the whole thing.

We stopped at the chicken zone, I had never ever seen so many chickens roaming around in fields and fields. "How do you find all the eggs?"

"See all the people walking around out there, they do it every day. They slowly walk through the fields looking for the eggs. These are the ones that go to market, as are most of the chickens. The chickens we actually keep to lay hatchlings are on the other side of the barns."

The barn is really not a good term. It was more like an enormous coup with tons of nesting ledges. But still, the chickens roam freely, but the ones who had laid eggs in their nests stayed with the nest. There were also baby chickens everywhere. And Roosters strutting their stuff.

"This is the most amazing thing I have ever seen. I didn't realize this was how chicken was raised and eggs were collected."

Truly

"It's not. We are completely free range, organic hormone free, and all natural. We aren't alone in this way, but we are one of the biggest in the world and absolutely the biggest in this part of the world."

We moved on to the buffalos. Kendall laughed at me when I exclaimed that they were Water Buffalo. "What did you think they were?"

"Well, you said buffalo, so I thought American type buffalo, like Bison."

He laughed for a long time about that, even told some of the workers who also started laughing. I guess I missed the humor.

The buffalo were much like the chickens. Free range. Large fields. The Breeding stock separate from the working stock separate from the food stock. But everything was very humane and surprisingly clean.

"So, would you like to ride one?"

"Oh No! No thank you, I AHHHHH!"

Just like that he picked me up and put me on top of a buffalo, then snapped a picture of me before I knew what was happening.

"Get me down you mongrel! Did Cera put you up to this?"

He helped me down and I slapped his chest. Him and his workers were laughing again, after I calmed down I laughed too. I can honestly say I had never sat on a water buffalo before!

Our final stop was at the rice paddies. These I had seen on the drive, but up close is a different experience. It was fun to see how the rice was actually harvested and to figure out what the people were actually doing out there. It was not so interesting actually, pulling weeks and checking plant health and readiness for harvest. I guess I should have known that too as much time as I spend in my own gardens doing exactly that.

Kendall took me back to the main house.

"Go clean up, you smell like a buffalo."

Jill Edick

"Hey!"

"Just being honest, you were the one who sat on one for a picture after all."

"Humph!"

"I will come for you in an hour. Dress your best, we have a fun night ahead of us!"

Then he was off.

Dress my best? There was nothing around here to dress up for, I was glad I brought a dress, but I still didn't understand. Men! The last great secret keepers!

As promised, he was back in one hour. I was barely dressed and ready, but he didn't seem to notice.

"Lena. Wow. You are the most beautiful woman I have ever seem. You look absolutely lovely."

I was having a hard time speaking to thank him. He looked amazing too. Perfectly tailored black slacks, a dark green button down shirt, black tie and Charcoal colored vest.

"Thank you Kendall. Might I reciprocate the complements. You look amazing. So very handsome."

"And I thank you my lady! Would you care to join me for dinner?"

He held out his arm and I took his elbow. I had my hand bag which I had stuck a couple of Cera's condoms, though not without some guilt. I didn't think I could cheat on Geoff. But I spent much of my wonderful morning thinking back over recent years and all the odd things that had been happening. Strange comments he had made. Weird late night phone calls. The money, the car. I started thinking about the bills and how I hadn't seen one for a long time. I had a household account that he put money into for groceries and kid stuff. But I never saw his paychecks or the other bills. Suddenly it started to dawn on me, that Geoff wasn't faithful to me. I confirmed this suspicion when I texted Cera this morning and asked her. She hadn't responded until about 20 minutes ago and the response was I'm so sorry Lena. I wondered how she knew, but I would find out I was quite certain.

But for tonight I decided I was going to enjoy the company of a handsome man who wanted to be with me. And if it went a little too far, so be it. I hadn't been loved in years. I couldn't remember the last time I had sex. I now understood why. And I made the decision to not let my life pass me by. I would deal with the farce that was my marriage when I got home.

Chapter 18

"Your very quiet tonight dear Lena. Penny for your thoughts?"

"Well, I was just wondering where we could be going out to."

"Who said out? I said dinner and dancing."

"You did indeed. So where are we having this dinner and dance?"

"The man cave."

"Your place? OK. Sounds interesting."

We were at his front door then and he opened it for me. There were flowers everywhere. Candles too. He had transformed his living room into a fancy dining space, nicer than any restaurant I had ever been too. The smell of something amazing was wafting in the air and set my mouth to watering.

"Wow. This is remarkable Kendall."

"Thank you. I hoped you would approve."

"How could I not? This is much better than some crowded restaurant. What is that smell? It is wonderful!"

"That is your dinner, fresh from the farm. I decided that I didn't want to share you with the rest of the world tonight. I don't know how much time I have left to enjoy your company, so I cleaned and cooked and now I don't have to share you with anyone. Tonight is ours."

I set my purse down and he pulled me into his arms. I hadn't noticed the music playing, but it was. We started dancing, slowly, pressed snugly into each other. I felt so alive. I had never danced this close to Geoff, never felt so cared for in his arms. In that moment I realized I had fallen head over heels in love with Kendall.

Suddenly he pulled away. "I think we better sit for dinner before I change my mind and let it burn."

I let him lead me to the table, but I was seriously considering telling him to let it burn. The strange thing was, that for the first time since I met Kendall, I felt absolutely no guilt at all.

I was sitting at the table while he went to retrieve our dinner.

First he brought out wine and filled our glasses, then went back for our plates. I offered to help and he flat out told me to sit. He brought out our plates which were brimming with rice and chicken.

"This looks great, what are we having?"

"Thai peanut chicken. The recipe is in the book my mom gave you. It was always a favorite of mine growing up, so I decided to share one of my favorite things with you. I hope you like it."

I didn't like it, I loved it. It was simply fabulous. I had tried Thai peanut chicken before in America actually, but I had never eaten anything like this. It was perfect.

"Kendall, this is wonderful! So simple and delicious. It is perfect!"

"Thank you. Wait until dessert."

"Oh my, what is that? I'm not sure I could eat another bite!"

"Well, shall we dance then and work our appetite back up?"

I think he was eluding to food, but his eyes twinkled with something else. My knees felt weak. I wasn't sure how I was going to stand and dance. Silly me, of course Kendall took care of that. Before I knew it I was up and in his arms slow dancing.

Jill Edick

He was so graceful and light on his feet, I reminded myself he didn't have a leg. How was he so beautiful on the dancefloor? It was like we were floating around the room. I completely forgot we were in his house. I was having such a great time. I could not think of one single time I had ever felt this good.

We were dancing and soon kissing. His hands were everywhere. I must admit, I finally gave in to temptation and ran my own hands down to that spectacular ass. He laughed and whispered, "Is it everything you hoped for?"

"And more. Shut up and kiss me!"

He didn't need to be told twice. Soon we were dancing into his room.

"Lena, I want you. I love you. Please, give me this night?"

"Yes, Kendall, yes, I'm yours. I love you too, please make love to me."

I was back in his arms again. The kiss was intense and deep. I felt the zipper of my dress going down and my dress fell to the floor.

He gently laid me back on his bed and stood up to start undressing himself.

"Lena, look at me please. I can do this with my prosthesis on, but it is better without. Are you ok with that?"

"Yes. I love you, there is nothing you can show me to stop that. Please do what is best."

"Oh Lena. Thank you. You are so amazing. How did I find you? How did I get so lucky? I love you!"

He leaned over and started kissing me again. When he next stopped he removed his vest, tie, shirt and slacks. What an amazing man. Absolutely beautiful. He unhooked his prosthesis then and balanced before me on his one leg so I could see him.

"Kendall. Your beautiful. Please, quite teasing."

He joined me on his bed then and we were kissing and touching and exploring each other. He had my bra off and across the room in no time.

"Kendall, wait,"

"What beautiful? Are you ok?"

"I'm perfect. But I need my purse. I'll be right back."

I jumped up before he could say a thing and ran to the living room and grabbed my purse and ran back to the bedroom where I literally flung myself into his arms. When we stopped kissing, I opened my purse and pulled out a condom.

He started laughing. "Did you really think I didn't have that taken care of? Your amazing Lena! You've been holding out. You wanted this as badly as I have you little minx."

"Oh yes, I wanted you since I first laid eyes on that ass."

We started kissing again and he had his hand in my panties and I let out a tremendous gasp and started to shudder.

I swear I heard bells.

"Lena, Lena honey, your phone. Do you need to check that?"

It took me a minute to register what he was saying. My phone? The bells! That was my phone, more specifically it was Cera. That was her ring tone. It started ringing again. She never called me over and over.

"I better get that. I'm so sorry."

"It's ok, I hope everything is all right."

"Cera! This better be an emergency!"

"Oh sweetie. I'm so sorry to interrupt you, I wouldn't if it weren't urgent."

"What? Are you ok? The girls? Jena? What's going on?"

"I'm ok, I just spoke to Jena and the girls are fine. But there was a police officer here just now looking to talk to you. They wouldn't tell me why. Said it was urgent the reach you immediately. I told them where you were then called Jana to check the girls. Lena, it must be Geoff. What else could it be?"

"Geoff? What could he want and why send cops?"

"No, honey, I think there is something wrong with Geoff."

There was a knock at Kendall's door. Neither of us were dressed to open it.

"Crap! Who is here?!" Kendall grabbed a pair of shorts, pulled them on and then grabbed a crutch by the bed I hadn't seen before and left the room.

"Someone just arrived at Kendall's place. Stay on the line Cera, I'm frightened."

"Of course I will. Set the phone down on speaker if you want."

I did. Then I started attempting to find articles of clothing I could put on. My bra was MIA and I couldn't put on the dress without one, so I grabbed Kendall's shirt and pulled it on. Fortunately, it was long enough to cover my rear.

"Lena, Honey, it's my lead security officer. He said he got a call from the police in Chiang Mai with a message to deliver to you. Why don't you finish dressing, I will put on some coffee. He can wait a few minutes." He tossed my bra at me. "Not that I don't like the choice of wardrobe, but since we have company…"

"Lena! Are you not dressed?"

"Holy crap! You startled me! Hi Cera, I didn't realize Lena had left the phone on. I think I will just leave now."

"Lena! Dammit. This really was a bad time. So what are you wearing that he likes?"

"Really Cera?"

"Sorry, sorry, inappropriate. I'm envisioning that you're in a swimsuit preparing to get in a hot tub, nothing else."

"Cera?"

"Yes sweetie,"

"I'm scared. What could the cops want with me so badly they found Kendall's head of security and sent him to me?"

"I don't know. But you're in good hands there. Kendall won't let anyone hurt you. And I'm not that far away. It'll be ok. Now are you out of that swimsuit and ready to go talk to the chief?"

"Yes. Thank you Cera. It's probably nothing, just some stupid mix up with the credit cards right?"

"I'm sure. Take the phone and go find out now. It'll be ok, I'll be right beside you no matter what."

I grabbed the phone and went to the living room.

Chapter 19

Kendall had his prosthesis back on when I made it to the living room, I never even saw him grab it.

I went and sat next to Kendall and set the phone down on the end table.

"Mrs. Jameson? I am Head of Security here, my name is Marcus." That didn't sound very Thai, but he didn't look very Thai.

"Hello Marcus, please call me Lena."

"Miss Lena. I am sorry to say that I have been given the job of sharing some bad news with you. It would seem that last night in New York, this morning sometime here, Mr. Geoffrey Jameson had a bit of a mishap. He unfortunately did not survive. I am so sorry Lena. Mr. Jameson has passed on."

Of all the things I had thought this could be, I honestly did not expect that. "A mishap Marcus? What kind of mishap? Was he in a traffic accident? Why did it take so long to notify me?"

From the phone I heard a gasp and some mumbling. "Cera? What is it?"

Marcus looked at Kendall and handed him a newspaper, a Wall Street Journal to be exact.

"Would someone please tell me what the hell is going on?"

"Oh Lena, I'm so sorry." Kendall was reading the paper. He looked up at Marcus then handed the paper to me.

"Lena, I'm here honey, I'm sorry, I was just re-reading the paper. I never thought it could be him. Oh my gosh."

Truly

I took the paper.

Prominent Stock Broker and suspect in the latest insider trading scandal found dead last night. The police have not yet confirmed his identity pending family notification. No details have been released on the death. Only that he was found in an ally not far from his prominent high rise apartment.

"Well this can't be him. He doesn't have a high rise apartment. He has a small loft on the New Jersey side of the river. It was less expensive but still an easy commute to his office. This can't be him. Insider trading? He would never do that! Cera, Cera, back me up, this is wrong, it isn't him. This is obviously a mistaken identity."

"Lena, honey, I'm so sorry. It's him, I'm positive. Remember that conversation we were going to have? Trust me on this, it's him. I only just found out about the insider trading before we left. I didn't want to ruin your trip. I was going to tell you before we went home. Honey, he was into some bad things. It sounds like it caught up to him. He must have been into this longer than I realized. I just started suspecting... god Lena, I'm so sorry. You have to know if I had known any sooner I would have told you."

"Oh Cera, how can it be?" I turned to Marcus. "How did he die? You didn't tell me."

"The NYPD are still investigating, but what I have been told is that they believe he was murdered."

"MURDERED? By who? Have they arrested anyone? Why did this take so long to get to me?"

"His body was just found a couple of hours ago. It took the police a bit to identify him and locate you. I have not heard about any arrests. Unfortunately, that is all the information I was given. I think it was all the Chiang Mai PD had as well. Please accept my condolences. I will take my leave now."

Kendall walked him out. He looked as stunned as I felt.

Jill Edick

"Lena? Kendall? I need to start making some travel arrangements. Are you coming back to Chiang Mai tonight or in the morning?"

"It is up to you Lena, I will take you back tonight if you want."

"When do you think we will be able to get a flight Cer?"

"I've been on the computer looking, I think the earliest I will be able to get us out of Chaing Mai is 8:00. That takes us to Bangkok. From there I don't think we will be able to get a flight until early afternoon and it looks like all that will be standby, there doesn't appear to be any seats available. But I need to call my company to let them know I will be leaving anyway, I will have our travel guru see if she can make something happen."

"Lena, why don't you go lie down. Let Cera and I work on the details. You aren't looking so good."

"Oh Lena, yes, go lie down. Might as well get a couple of hours of rest if you can. I will let Kendall know of the arrangements as soon as I know something."

"Yes, I need to use the restroom. I will lay down after." I was in such a state of shock I really didn't even comprehend what I just said.

Chapter 20

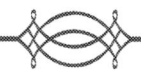

I Know I must have been in shock. I went into the bathroom and started filling Kendall's tub and climbed in before it was even half full. Geoff was dead. He was involved in illegal activities. He got himself murdered. I was so confused and I felt so stupid that I never realized the things that were going on in my own life. How long had this been going on? How was this going to affect me and the girls? Had I cried yet? I didn't think so. How was I feeling about this? I had been about to make love with another man and then found out my husband had been murdered. Was that my punishment for being unfaithful? Surely not, but why, why did this happen?

I heard a knock on the door and Kendall peeked in.

"Lena? Are you ok? Can I get you anything?"

"You can come in. No I don't need anything. I just felt so cold. I think it's shock but I decided I needed a bath. I hope you don't mind."

"You are welcome to my tub any time. I brought you a cup of tea. I'm sure you are in shock. I'm so sorry Lena. Can I help you with anything?"

"No. I'm just trying to process this. I just don't understand. How could this be? Am I that naïve? How did I not know things were going on? I just feel so stupid and hurt and scared. What do I tell my girls? How do I go on, I have no idea what our bills even look like. And am I a bad person because I'm more worried about all of that than how he died? I loved Geoff, one upon a time a lot. But I came to the realization that I really haven't loved him the past few years, at all. But he's still the girl's father and we had a life together no matter how pathetic it was. Why can't I seem to muster up even a single tear for him?"

"Oh Lena, you are crying. You have been since Marcus gave you the news. You are definitely in shock. Do I need to warm up the water at all? I want to hug you, hold you, make it all right."

"I want that too. Please, can you join me? I just want to be held, not talk, nothing else, just be held and feel loved."

He didn't even hesitate. He took off his prosthesis, got undressed and slid into the tub behind me without a word. He wrapped his arms around me and just held me. It was perfect. It was then I realized I was crying, and I started sobbing. He just held me tighter and combed his fingers in my hair. All the while whispering sweet words of love in my ear. It was then I realized, I would be ok. I had an amazing best friend who would help me. I was strong and smart; I could do this. And maybe even someday soon I would get to see Kendall again and never feel guilty about it. I would deal with that in time as well. I love him, I know it now more than ever and I believe he loves me too. It was going to be all right. My crying slowed down and I got my breathing under control.

"Kendall?"

"Yes my love?"

"I don't' want to leave yet. Is that wrong? Do we have to go back to Chiang Mai tonight?"

"No we don't. Your friend is defiantly a miracle worker, but even she wasn't a match for the airlines. The first flight she could even get a standby ticket wasn't until day after tomorrow. So if you want to spend the night, you are absolutely welcome. I will take you back when your ready tomorrow. Cera said she would drive you guys back to Bangkok and she has a room near the airport lined up. Hopefully she will get you on flights the next day then."

"Kendall?"

"Yes my love?"

"Thank you."

"Of course. You should probably call Cera and let her know when she can expect you, she will be worrying I'm sure."

"Kendall?"

"Am I sensing a trend here? Yes my love?"

"Would you mind letting Cera know I'm ok? I just don't want to talk about that stuff anymore tonight."

"Of course. Would you like me to stay here awhile longer or go do that now?"

"Please hold me for a while longer. This is so nice."

I cuddled into him. He was built so solidly, but was still comfortable. We fit together so nicely. It was like we were built to fit with each other. The longer I stayed there in his arms the more comfortable I felt, and something else. The stress of the evening must be messing with my brain function. I was so wanting to be held by him, but not here, I needed to feel him. Love him. Surely this was the most inappropriate thing I could be thinking about. But my brain kept saying this is normal, go with it. My heart said listen to your brain, I may never say that again as your brain is usually wrong.

"Kendall?"

"Yes my love?"

"I think I'm ready for bed."

"Of course. You must be exhausted. Why don't you get out. I'll be out shortly. It takes me a bit longer to get out of the tub. You would be helping me much if you would lay out some towels on the floor for me so I don't slip."

I got out of the tub and wrapped a towel around myself, then spread several on the floor.

"You can take the bed Lena, I will sleep on the couch. Let me know if you need a fan or anything."

"Thank you Kendall."

I went to the bedroom and put on a nighty and climbed into bed. I heard Kendall leave the bathroom a few minutes later and settle down in the living room.

I thought I was tired and would fall right to sleep what with the stress and all. But all I could think about was Kendall. How kind he had been. How nice it was to lean on him and be held in his arms in the tub. The sweet words he whispered to me. The feelings he had brought out in me before the phone rang. None of that had changed I realized. My life was no doubt on a fast moving roller coaster that I couldn't control, but I still had this night. I wanted this night. I needed this night.

I got out of bed and went to the living room. I could see Kendall laying on the couch, but he didn't look like he was having any better luck sleeping that I had had. I walked over in front of the sofa. He looked up at me.

"Kendall?"

"My love?"

I leaned down and he sat up and we met in the middle in a needy, strong kiss. He wrapped his arms around my waist and I straddled his lap.

"Oh Lena, are you sure?"

"Yes, please Kendall, I need this, I need you."

He had my panties in his hands and pulled off me so quickly I barely felt them come off. I don't know when he took his pants off. The next thing I felt was him thrust up into me. His hands on my hips guiding me down onto him as he thrust. His lips found my breast and was love biting my nipple with his teeth. My arms were around his neck and he started pulling me harder and faster onto him. Suddenly he had me up and flipped onto my back and he took control. I was whimpering. I never ever had sex like this. The intensity was mind blowing and at that thought I let out a scream and had the most intense orgasm I had ever had. Kendall's lips found mine and he started thrusting even faster as I was crying out in between kisses. Then he was coming with me. With a final cry he collapsed on top of me. I wrapped my arms around his neck and we lay there together coming down from the clouds.

"Lena."

"Kendall."

"I'm so sorry."

"Sorry? Whatever for?"

"That was absolutely not how I intended out first time to be."

"I wasn't complaining."

"I'm not complaining. I just really wanted our first time making love to be softer…slower…I don't know, I just feel like I could have made that so much better for you."

"I don't know how you could have made that better. But I will certainly let you give it another try."

He did not need any further encouragement. He rose, grabbed his crutch in one arm, and my hand with his other and led me to the bedroom.

Chapter 21

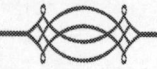

We woke up the next morning and the reality of what was to come washed over me. I needed to get back home. I needed to talk to the girls and tell them their dad had passed away. I had a funeral to arrange. And a life to figure out. As wonderful as the night before was, it was time to return to the world of cold hard reality.

"I can tell your ready to get moving. I'm going to go make us some breakfast while you shower."

He got up then and left the room for me to get up and going.

After breakfast he walked me back up to the main house to pack up my belongings while he got cleaned up himself. We were on the road an hour later. I had talked to Cera, and there was still no change in the travel options. But she was working on it.

"Lena?"

"Kendall?

"Would you like me to go with you? I could help you I'm sure. If nothing else be a support."

"Oh Kendall. I would love that, I really would. But I think I better go by myself for now. The girls are going to be shocked. And I have no idea what I'm looking at for investigations and bills. I guess I just need to figure things out first before I introduce you to the equation. Plus, you have your business here. I don't want to keep you from that either."

"My business is fine with me or without. But I understand. Your about to have a whole life change. One thing at a time. But you need to know, I will be there in a heartbeat if you need me. My word."

Truly

"Thank you Kendall. You have no idea how much that means to me."

When we arrived in Chiang Mai, Cera was still not having any luck finding flights out. We were on standby for tomorrow but it wasn't looking good. I got on the phone with the detective in NY to inquire about the investigation. There were a few leads, but my husband (I kept thinking of him as Husband, but really ex-husband sounded better. I wondered if I could divorce a dead person) had so many enemies with the scandal that they were having a lot of investigating to do. Besides the murder investigation, the White Collar crimes division was investigating the insider trading mess. They had frozen our bank accounts and all means of money I could access. The only account they had not yet frozen was my personal account. But there was nothing in it, so that wasn't going to help me.

"Don't worry Lena, you know I will help you. You can pay me back much later."

"That doubles for me, no payback required."

"Thanks you two. I'm sure I'll be fine, but it's good to know I will have help if I need it. Lord knows my mom won't help I'm sure. No doubt she will find a way to blame the whole mess on me somehow."

"I'm all packed up Lena. Why don't you go get packed up. We can head to Bangkok when you're ready."

I had the feeling she was wanting to get rid of me to talk to Kendall, but I didn't really care at that moment. I just knew I needed to get home, so I went in and packed up all my belongings. I wasn't sure how we were going to get some of it home. I had a lot of wine. We had originally planned to ship it, but had not gotten that done yet. Maybe Kendall could take it and ship it to us. I had also planned to ship a bunch of souvenir things that wouldn't fit in my suitcases. Maybe I could just buy another suitcase and pay the extra baggage fee.

Then I stopped. Here I was worrying about things. Geoff had been murdered. I had no idea by whom, or how or really why. Were the girls and I safe? That was what I should be worrying about. I sat down on my bed and couldn't help it, the tears started again. I fell onto my side and cried. Awhile later I heard someone come in. Cera laid down next to me and hugged me to her.

"I'm so sorry Lena. I can't even begin to imagine. Just cry honey, I'm here. I'm not going anywhere."

I was so lucky to have her. How was I going to survive without her when she had to leave for some work adventure?

I didn't realize I had voiced that out loud until she answered.

"I spoke with my employer. I had actually talked with them about this before which is why I have been training assistants on the last few trips. I love seeing new places, but I am ready to not have to travel all the time. I want to travel for fun, not work. I'm ready to lay down some roots and maybe even meet my own Mr. wonderful. I'm ready to be home. So I have been working on becoming the liaison for the traveling employees, helping them coordinate meetings, and get access to land, finding places to eat and where to visit when traveling. I never had that. Most of us haven't, and it has been challenging to travel blind while still having to accomplish the job. The company is learning and researching so much, we really need more people traveling and collecting samples and researching. To do that, there really needs to be better assistance to those in the field. That's what I'm going to do. It wasn't supposed to happen until the beginning of next year, but in light of events, I asked to move that date up. I feel like I need to be here for you. My job will allow me to work from anywhere, so I can be with you helping."

"Congratulations Cera! How wonderful for you."

"Thank you. I'm very excited. And I'm glad I will be around for you and the girls."

"Is Kendall still here?"

"He left to go to his place for a while to try to help us somehow. I don't, he was vague. Said he would be back in an hour or less."

Truly

"Do you think he can take that stuff on the table over there for me and ship it? I don't think I can take that much wine on the plane and through customs back home."

"I'm sure he can handle that. Actually, I have some stuff too."

She jumped up and ran out of the room. Hurricane Cera on the move.

I got up and washed my face and finished packing stuff up. I was just finishing when I heard Cera talking in the other room so I went to see if Kendall was back.

"You are amazing! No wonder Lena fell so hard for you! Thank you Kendall!"

"It is my pleasure. Really."

"What's going on out here?"

"Oh Lena, it's great news! Kendall is going to let us use the company plane to get home. We can leave soon and will be able to get home faster."

"Really? Oh Kendall! Thank you!" I threw myself into his arms.

"Well, just so you know, a company employee must stay with the plane, so I guess you will be stuck with me, at least until you get to the United States. I hope you don't mind being around me awhile longer. And before either of you start envisioning great private jets, let me remind you, our business involves live stock. We have to have an economical way of shipping product, and in some cases animals. There is a comfortable area for us humans, but most of the plane is dedicated to shipping things. It's not a fancy plane, but it will get you home."

"I don't care if I have to ride with a bunch of chickens. Thank you Kendall. How can I repay you?"

"You don't, this is my pleasure. Really Lena, I have the means to do this and I want to. It's what you do when you love someone."

"This plane of yours can leave Chiang mai?" Cera sounded a little skeptical.

"True, it is a small airport. I won't lie, the take off and landings here with that big of a plane is a bit alarming, but we do it a lot and our pilots are good. You're in good hands. Promise."

He started looking around to see the amount of stuff we had packed. "Well, next problem. Everything should be fine except the wine. You will never get through customs with that much wine and we are an agriculture shipping plane, so I don't think we can justify bringing alcohol into the country. How about if I take that with me, and I will ship it so you?"

"Thank you again Kendall. Your amazing."

"Do we need to take the rental car anywhere special Cera?"

"No, my assistant is staying here as well and he is keeping the car to finish up the job. I'm ready to go."

"Lena, you need anything else?"

"No. I'm ok."

"Well, then, the plane should be ready and I have a car waiting to take us there. Shall we?"

We called for a bell hop and left the hotel for the last time. As we left I looked over at the garden, the place where Kendall and I had watched the stars. Would I ever see those stars the same way again?

Part 3

One of the hardest things in life is having words
in your heart that you can't utter

James Earl Jones

Chapter 22

Kendall was correct that the takeoff was a bit hairy, but we got up in the air and were headed home in no time. Cera found a chair, plugged in her ear phones and brought up her computer. I sat with Kendall and fell asleep leaning on his shoulder.

I woke a couple hours later feeling totally disoriented.

"Hey beautiful. Are you hungry? You haven't eaten anything since breakfast. You should eat something. We don't have a lot of stuff on the plane, but there are a few things. I can go get you something."

"Sure, I guess I could eat something."

He got up, stopped to talk to Cera for a minute then disappeared. He came back a few minutes later with drinks and snacks for both Cera and I.

"We will be in San Diego in about 8 hours. We have to stop there to refuel. We will go through customs then to save some time before we head to Denver. Cera says she will have a car waiting for you to go see your girls. She said she wants to stay overnight there. Get through some jet lag and give you a chance to talk to the girls and make some decisions. I can fly you on home the next day if you want. There is plenty of room for the girls too. If you would prefer to go on alone to see how things are before bringing them into it, that's fine too. Just let me know so we can file flights plans."

I sighed heavily. I hadn't really thought about how to tell the girls and whether or not they should go home with me. Who knows what was going to happen when I got home. So many things to think about. No wonder I was so disoriented. "I'm just so confused and discombobulated. I have no idea what to tell the girls. Your dad was murdered just doesn't sound good. But I don't want to lie either. Thank you for staying and letting us continue to use your plane. Where will you stay?"

"The crew and I will stay at a hotel near the airport. Don't worry about us. We are old hands at this. I don't know that I am the best person to give you advice on the girls. Maybe you should go talk with Cera for a while. I have some work to do, so don't worry that I will get to lonely." He kissed my cheek.

I went over to talk with Cera and shared my worries.

"I have been thinking about that as well. You can't lie to them. Telling them there was an accident won't work. Plus, they aren't stupid and can read a paper. This is going to have a lot of fall out. Jena has kept the news off and gotten rid of newspapers, but she says this is already making nationwide news. When they get home kids will act like kids do, which is like little assholes, so what they don't know from you they will hear from other kids. No doubt there will be a lot of hate aimed your direction as well. From what Jena has been telling me and I have been reading online, the majority of people are being quite sadistic and saying he got what he deserved. I was kind of thinking maybe it would be better for the girls to stay with my sister for a while longer under the cover of anonymity."

"My god! People say he deserved this? How does anyone deserve to be killed? I don't even know what he did. Maye it's time you told me what you know Cera."

"Shit. Okay. I suspected years ago he was having an affair. I don't know if you realize quite when the dynamics of your relationship changed, but it did. I saw it, even Lindy saw it. She emailed me and asked me once why daddy never came home any more. I hired an investigator. It wasn't pretty. He was carrying on with multiple women. He wasn't living in that tiny flat you two rented. He moved up town to some swanky apartment. I confronted him. I went to his office and lit him up. He actually cried. He begged me not to tell you. He said he was working all these hours and trying to build up his retirement portfolio so he could retire sooner and spend time with you. He insisted he loved you, he was just lonely. The women were just one night stands and he used protection. He would never hurt you and the girls. I told him if he was trying so hard to save money, why the big ass apartment, why not stay in the affordable flat. He said he entertains a lot of business partners and clients and needed a better place to do that. I suggested a fucking restaurant. He broke down again. Said I was right of course and he would call his realtor and list the apartment and find something else. He literally got on his knees and begged me not to tell you. I agreed but only because I didn't want to see you hurt. He seemed so genuinely remorseful. It was a side of that asshole I had never seen. Imagine how stupid I felt when I discovered how good of an actor he really was."

"When… when was this?"

"About two and a half years ago."

"What happened? Things didn't get better for us. There must be more."

"Unfortunately. I was stupid and wanted to believe the snake. I never followed up. About a year ago I got wind of some miracle stockbroker making a name for himself and millions for his clients. I was updating my personal portfolio and really didn't like the broker we used at work. So I started researching investment advisors to see if I could find someone to help me like Mr. miracle was. Low and behold, guess who Mr. miracle was? The hairs on the back of my neck stood up. I called my investigator and set him to work. The things he told me were alarming at best. He had listed his apartment alright. But not to downgrade. He moved to a penthouse and bought it, not rented it. He had a car garage with five, yes five very expensive imports. His womanizing hadn't stopped; they just became more expensive call girls. The investigator started to dig into finances and things were not adding up right. Try as we might, we could not reconcile where he was getting the money for the lifestyle he was living. You may remember, about that time I started asking how you were doing financially. You seemed completely clueless to what was going on, and even more separated from Geoff. I wanted to tell you then, but I couldn't get past the money. I was afraid if I told you there would be a giant mess and you would be the one to come out destitute."

She stopped then and went to her bag to grab out a bottle of wine she had brought with her since we could bring some wine through customs with us. She opened it and didn't bother with glasses. She sat down with me again and took a long drink then passed me the bottle. "Drink, you're going to need it to forgive me for what I'm going to tell you next."

I drank all right. I wasn't mad at Cera, what could she have possibly found out and not told me that would make me mad at her? I was furious with Geoff though. He was just an ass, Cera was trying to protect me. Although if I was being honest with myself, I wish she would have told me. I understood why she did what she did, but it should have been my decision how to proceed. "Tell me."

"I decided I was going to go to him with my investment needs. Nowhere near my entire portfolio. But a couple thousand dollars. I never told him I had investigated him again. I just went in like a client. He said he could turn my thousands into millions inside of a year. I was shocked. How could you do that I asked. Because he is smarter than the average investor he told me. His portfolio didn't lie, that's for sure. It didn't make sense, but the fact was he was making money hand over fist. So I gave him the money and continued to have him investigated. For a couple of months my money was growing leaps and bounds. It was amazing. I almost forgave his inability to not be an asshole and give him the rest of my money. Thank god I didn't. The investigator came up with a good amount of dirt about then. The hookers had suddenly dried up. Unfortunately, one of the cutesy little company receptionists moved in with Geoff in the penthouse. She quit her job, started dressing better, driving a fancy ass car, and living high on the hog in Geoff's penthouse. Perhaps Geoff should have had her investigated. She was married. No divorce on record, but no outward signs of a husband either. I was about to go to him with this information when I got a statement in the mail for my investments. I lost everything. Everything he had made me plus what I had originally invested. I called that fucker all right. He assured me it was just a little snag; the money would be back not to worry. I asked how he intended to make the money back with no money to invest. Son of a bitch actually told me I should give him another $5000. I told him to go to hell. And if he was lucky there would be a penthouse there with his little live in whore. I hung up on him and intended to call you next. Mind you I was in another country at the time and actually had my own job to do. I decided to wait until I got back state side and come tell you in person with all the proof I had. Bastard must have finally figured out that you can hire investigators, because he somehow got my flight schedule and had a goon waiting for me at the airport. He threatened my sister and her kids. Threatened my job and the rest of my money. Said he would take down my company and all the money in it. To make a point, the company's stock crashed the next day. It recovered and our jobs were ok, but most of the employees lost a shit ton of money. I don't know how he did it. My investigator called me the next day and quit, he returned my deposit and never sent me another bill. Geoff called me a week later and all he said was 'any questions bitch?' and hung up. I didn't know what to do. I wanted to choose you, I really did. Your my best friend and like a sister to me. But if I didn't back off, he was going to destroy hundreds of lives. I was absolutely sick. I texted him back 'no questions prick.' I had no idea the extent of what he was doing. I was sure it wasn't legal, but I couldn't prove anything. I wanted to tell you, but again I was afraid it would backfire and you and the girls would be the ones to suffer. I didn't do anything. I am totally ashamed of myself. Totally sick. I lived with it for months. I decided the best thing to do was to help you find your own way out of that fucked up relationship. So I bought you the trip. I hoped you would have such an amazing time and once away from home you would start to figure some things out on your own. I never imagined how the trip would go. And in my wildest dreams I never envisioned what would happen back home while we were gone."

Throughout the entire talk we had somehow managed to finish the bottle of wine. Kendall showed up with another one and three glasses. By the look on his face he had heard everything.

"Do you still have all the investigators notes Cera?"

"Yes of course. And copies. After the threats started I made a dozen copies of everything and put them all in secure locations."

"Do you have the name of your investigator?"

"Yes. But he won't return my calls any longer. I believe his exact words to me the last time we talked was 'never contact me again, I like my life and my family and my money, please disappear from my life.' I haven't tried to contact him since. I'm thinking I need to go to the police with all this information when we get back to PA. I'm thinking I need to contact him and tell him to do the same."

"Absolutely you both do. But we can't forget that there is a murderer out there. Obviously someone close to this situation somehow. I'm concerned about your safety. Both of you. Lena, I know you didn't want to bring me into the family dynamic quite yet. I respect that. But you are the woman I love and I intend to spend the rest of my life with you and be a father to your girls that their own obviously was incapable of. I will not sit by and let something happen to any of you, Cera you too! I'm going to make some calls and get some security put into place for you both. Until such a time as the security is properly in place Lena, there is no chance in hell I am leaving you. You can introduce me as Cera's assistant, manager, body guard, I don't care, but I'm not leaving you two unprotected. I think the shit storm that is about to come is going to be ugly and ultimately devastating. Once security is in place and the initial wave a shit has settled, I will return to Thailand to deal with my own business. Fair enough?"

Cera and I were both crying. Where did I find this man again and how did I get so lucky? Cera was able to speak first.

"Thank you Kendall. I can of course pay for my own security, but I would welcome your assistance in finding someone good." She turned toward me, "Lena, I think you need to leave the girls with my sister awhile longer. You need to tell them the truth, that their dad was killed and there is an investigation ongoing. Until they find the person who did this, you need them to be safe. We can introduce Kendall as a private investigator who is helping you and assisting the police with their investigation. None of that is a lie, just a little easier of a pill to swallow. Plus, they should feel some comfort that there are people working on this and you will be safe when you return to PA without them."

"I agree with Cera. I unfortunately cannot stay indefinitely, yet anyway, but I can and will be here until we make sure there is protection in place. I think getting an attorney on retainer immediately should be a high priority, and I agree Cera you need to get info to the police. It could help them find the person who did this. Do you know of any good personal attorneys we can contact from San Diego?"

"I do. I actually have a great attorney that helps me with lots of odds and end things. I will call him and see if he can recommend someone in the PA area who can help us."

"Make sure whoever it is, they are a Pitbull! If this turns as ugly as it has potential for, Lena will need a rabid fighter."

"Hold on, wait, a lawyer? For what, I didn't do anything?"

"Well certainly you did not murder Geoff. However, you were his wife and the fallout from the trading scandal is going to hit you in some way. There just isn't any way around that. How badly it hurts you will depend on how bad the trading mess is and how good of an attorney you get. You need to brace yourself. This will not be easy."

I was so overwhelmed. What the hell had Geoff gotten me into? I wasn't even over the fact that he was gone, dead. I hadn't even told the girls yet, there was no funeral, and already my life was in chaos. I felt sick. I got up and ran for the bathroom and threw up. When I was done, I just sat on the floor crying.

Kendall came and sat down next to me. "I'm so sorry honey. I can't even imagine how you are feeling right now. I don't mean to make it harder, but I do want you safe."

"I know. I know. I appreciate everything you're doing. I am just so overwhelmed. Shocked."

"I can understand that. I can also say conclusively that Cera is taking this super hard. She is blaming herself and is afraid you hate her."

"I don't blame her! I could never hate her!"

"Tell her that. You two need each other now."

He helped me off the floor and we went out to where Cera was sitting with tears running down her cheeks.

"Oh Cer! You know I don't hate you! I never could! You were in an impossible position. What's done is done, I need you now. I have no idea what is coming, and I'm scared. Please don't check out on me."

She jumped up and hugged me. Somehow we would get through this right? We had to.

Chapter 23

When we landed in San Diego, Cera was on the phone with her attorney right away. Kendall was on the phone with someone speaking in rapid Thai, then he disappeared to talk with crew.

Cera was done first. "He is going to look into some attorneys for us. He will call me with some names by the time we get to Denver."

"I just still can't believe all of this. What the hell happened to Geoff? Why did he do these things that probably got him killed? That's what bothers me most. Why?"

"We may never know Lena. He got caught up in the money probably, the dream of easy riches. Who knows."

"Okay ladies. The plane has cleared customs, we are refueled and ready to go. Ready to see the girls?"

We took off. Once in the air Cera asked Kendall what his calls were about.

"I was talking to my security guys. They're looking into some options for us in PA. I also contacted one of my attorneys. He has some colleagues here in the US that he is going to contact as well. I'm hoping to have some security in place and a couple of good attorneys on retainer before we even land in PA. I also spoke with our marketing director. She's a wiz. She said she has actually been following this whole thing online and says there is an enormous news presence involved. We should be expecting them to know when you return Lena. The only plus we have going here is that we are on a private plane and not traveling on the original date you were booked. However, there will still be a presence of the media in wait at the airport and there is really no way to avoid it. Once they see you, it is going to start raining. Enjoy tonight. Your about to get your 15 minutes whether you want them or not."

"Hell! They won't know about us arriving in CA or moving on to CO will they?"

"They shouldn't. I was originally going to have you both clear customs in San Diego as well, but decided against it. No one knows you're here right now and that is good. You won't have a choice in Denver. The plane is good so we can land and get you off quickly, but as soon as you hit customs, the flag will go up. After customs though we should be able to get you out of the airport quickly, no need for baggage claim and a car should be waiting. Tomorrow coming back though will be a different story. Once they figure out how you got here, they will just have to look up our flight plans and the media will be everywhere. They are probably already staking out your place Cera just in case you show up there. My thinking is that we skip your place Cera. I can have your belongings delivered there for you if you like. I think we should just leave your bags in the back here though. They went through the customs screening, so it's just you two and your belongings up here you have to take. If we leave most of it here, we can move faster. Then we should go directly to your sisters Cera. That will throw off the scent for a while. You may want to encourage your sister to go away for a while with the kids. The media should leave her alone once you both leave, but who knows how they will behave. Vultures."

"I just don't get it, we're not famous or anything."

"Lena, like it or not your news. And Kendall, do you think you should be seen with us? It's one thing that we are in your company's plane, that is going to put you in this spotlight already, but the heir to the company escorting the wife of the murdered crook may not be the publicity you want."

"No, your right Cera. That's why I called our marketing people and attorney. They are preparing statements as we speak. I am however something of a recluse in the media eye. I sincerely doubt the American media will be able to pick me out of a crowd of two. That said, we are going to leave the plane separately. Lena is going to go first with one of my plane security guys. He will be with her all the way to the car. The car will leave without us Lena. But you will be safe, I promise. We need to throw off the scent though for the safety of your kids. I'm not going to be too far behind. I will go through the airport with all the 'unknowns' acting just as baffled as the rest of them. I am taking a cab to a meeting place and we will reconnect when it is private enough to do so. Cera will be leaving the plane with our co-pilot well after Lena. Again, if they don't see you two together perhaps they will not piece together any thoughts of your sister and it will buy you some time and keep the kids out of the spot light. There will be another car for you Cera. It will take you direct to your sisters. Lena and I will arrive shortly after you. Hopefully we can avoid at least the worst of the media's invasion for tonight. I have plans for tomorrow already worked out. I'm sorry Lena, you will not get to spend a lot of time with the girls tonight, but I really think it's for the best. I know I told you earlier to let me know about the girls, but I figured it was pretty consensual after the earlier conversation that they should stay here until things calm down. So I have a flight plan made, the pilot will submit it at the very last minute."

Wow, he got a lot done in a short time.

"Why does Lena have to go first?"

"Simple, she will draw the media off of you and I. My guy will get her to the car safely, I promise. But once she has them distracted you won't be anyone of interest and that's good. If they don't see you with her, they won't immediately look at your sister place."

"Are you sure this is safe? I always thought safety in numbers you know."

"She will be safe Cera, I promise. Lena, trust me?"

"Of course Kendall. I won't lie and say I'm not nervous, but I will do what you say. The girls need to be kept out of this frenzy. It should be illegal for them to harass the kids."

The captain came over the speaker then. We were approaching Denver. Cera and I got our carry on's ready and sat back for the landing. Each of us in our own thoughts for what was about to happen. How was it possible that just hours ago we were in Thailand? Where did the time and the trip go so quickly?

We touched down and I started freaking out a bit.

"Lena, honey, you need to calm down. Here, put on this cap and your sun glasses. Keep them on until you have to take them off for customs, then get them back on and stay with Kiet. Do what he says and go where he tells you. Don't talk to anyone but customs and keep your head down. It will be over soon."

As soon as he finished telling me this he kissed me. Not a frenzied kiss like last night, but still just as intense. It helped. He helped. I can't imagine if we had been on a commercial flight and doing this without help.

Then who I was assuming was Kiet appeared and took my carry-on bag leaving me with my purse. He took my elbow and led me off the plane. The walk to customs wasn't bad. We got through fairly quickly. We were approaching baggage when I saw a few people with cameras and mic's. Kiet steered me over near a baggage claim area that was packed with people waiting for bags. We went around them and got to the exit door before anyone was the wiser. When the door swished open though, my hat blew off and someone immediately yelled 'Darlena Jameson!' Kiet had my elbow and was walking me very quickly out the doors to the curb for pick up. Airport security arrived then and pushed back the oncoming wave of media, giving us a bit of a head start. Kiet turned me away from the doors and picked up the pace. As we passed each door, there was media people running along inside and snapping pictures through the doors. Some had gotten past security and were outside now chasing me down. Suddenly we stopped and Kiet opened a car door and shoved me in, tossed my bag in behind me, then slammed the door and the car took off. I didn't even have my seatbelt fastened and before we were off.

"Good evening ma'am. For now, please keep your head down. There is another cap back there, wanted to be prepared. When I tell you, put it on and sit up then buckle up."

Truly

"Okay" was all I managed to squeak out.

We drove for a couple of minutes before he told me to sit up. I did with the cap on. I buckled up then looked out the window. There were three cars just like the one I was in with a woman in a cap in each one. Sure enough when I looked behind me, there were news vans catching up quickly.

"Hang on ma'am. This could be an interesting ride. On the floor back there is a box. Take a couple of the things out and put them up in the car for me please."

There was a stuffed dog in there which I tossed in the back window and several decal things, so I grabbed one and put it on the side window. I noticed the women in the other cars had been doing the same thing.

We were approaching an exit and two of the cars took the exits, us and another car kept going but started separating in the traffic. At the next exit the other car took off. We continued straight past the next couple turns then we too turned and started working our way towards downtown. I couldn't tell if anyone was still following me, but I didn't look to hard, I didn't want to be obvious.

We finally made it to downtown Denver and all of its confusing one ways. Our driver took a call and said 2 minutes. We were approaching the 16th street mall when he pulled over, turned around, handed me a $20 and said to go to Starbucks and wait.

I thanked him, took my bag and purse and got out. I could see Starbucks not to far away and started walking in that direction. It was then I noticed 2 more women in caps and sunglasses walking around. But I still didn't see any sort of media.

A small red car pulled up next to me then and the window went down.

"Going my way?"

It was Kendall. I jumped in. "What about Starbucks and the $20?"

"If there had been any media I wouldn't have stopped. I would have come got you after the other diversions led the media in the wrong direction. Just another precaution. You lost them pretty quickly though. I am not sure Cera got so lucky. I wasn't counting on Airport Security to hold up the media, so they were still milling about when Cera came through. I reset the diversionary cars to help her and they will come this way too, where the diversions down here are if the media follows her this far. You and I however are getting out of here."

This was crazy! It was like a strange movie!

My phone started ringing.

"DON'T ANSWER!"

"Whoa! Sorry, I won't. Geesh."

"Sorry, I don't mean to yell, It's probably some media outlet. They may even have trackers that can find you if you use it. Your better just turning it off for now. Once your back in PA you can use it, but here, I wouldn't, don't want to risk it."

I turned it off and put it back in my purse. Stupid thing was almost dead anyway and the charger was back on the plane.

"I'm sorry Lena, I really didn't mean to yell at you. I just never even thought to tell you about the phone. I hope Cera doesn't answer hers. Damn, what else did I not think of."

"Kendall, your being too hard on yourself. I'm ok, Cera is smart, she'll be fine too. I can't ever thank you enough for everything you have done. How did you organize all of this? If you hadn't been here, I would still be back at the airport getting mugged while waiting for my bags at baggage claim. You are my hero! Thank you for this. I love you!"

"I love you Lena! I can't wait to tell the world. In your time of course."

"I will let you know. One thing at a time though for now. What are we going to be going through tomorrow to get back to the airport?"

"Well that will actually be easier in Denver. Once we get there we just have to get to security to lose the media. After that it'll be easy until we get in to PA. I hope we will have security set up to meet us and attorneys to handle the media."

"That will be nice. Let someone else handle the nonsense! I'm so glad to have you here with me."

"Lena, if security is in place, I won't be joining you getting off the plane in PA. Cera was right, I did not think when I offered up the plane, but I can't risk damaging my father's good name. I love you, and I will go to the ends of the earth for you, but I also love my family and I can't hurt them either. It's one thing to say you and Cera chartered our plane to get home, it's another to have me being involved in all this. If there is a way I can keep you safe and my family protected, I have to do that. So if security is in place, I won't be joining you. Obviously if they are not, I will not throw you to the wolves, that will never happen."

"Oh, well of course. Makes sense. I understand."

"Lena…"

"No, Kendall, really I understand. I'm just disappointed. But I understand. You have already put yourself way out there and it's bad enough my husband was such a shit, there is no reason you should be associated with that. I wish I didn't have to be. It's ok."

"Lena, please listen to me."

"Kendall, really I understand."

"Lena! Listen please! I love you. This mess with your husband does not change that! But we both have to protect ourselves and the people we love. How would it look for you to come back from a short trip with a lover while your husband was being murdered in the middle of a scandal here? And you have kids to think about. I'm not leaving you. Ever! You are stuck with me, that is my vow to you! But we need separation while this thing gets dealt with. I'm only a phone call or e-mail or skype away.

I will help you any way you need. But it will be with me in my corner of the earth and you in yours."

I was crying. I really did understand, but I felt like I was losing him. And I never really had him. It was devastating.

The car pulled over. Kendall put the car in park and turned to me.

"Lena. We are never that far apart. Ever! I vow to you right now, I will continue to share my stars with you. Every Thursday night at 10:00 like I promised, I will be outside. I will be looking up and sharing the stars with you! Every single night if I can! When I need you I will know you are there with me in the stars! Will you join me?"

I looked at him, still crying. I couldn't find my voice. I shook my head yes. He kissed me.

"Are we ok love?"

I shook my head again.

I looked around and realized we were in Boulder. We were almost there. I needed to get my head together. I was about to tell the kids about their father.

Chapter 24

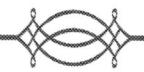

We drove up the road a ways father then pulled over and parked again. This was the meeting spot for Cera. We didn't have to wait long. They pulled up and she got out and joined us in our car.

"Well that was an adventure. I would prefer not to do that again."

We all got a chuckle out of that. It wasn't the best of situations, but at least Cera had found some way to make us smile for a minute.

"Well ladies, we are almost there. How do we want to do this?"

"I think I will just go in and after the initial 'your home yay' stuff introduce you as Cera's assistant, you came along with us to offer assistance with a difficult situation. That seems logical enough, and then I will tell them. I don't see any point to putting it off."

"Do you want me there Lena?"

"Of course. They will need us both Cera. Jena too if she will stay."

"Ok, Driver take us onward then."

"Driver? It's a good thing I like you Cera or I would dump your arse out right here."

We all chuckled again. Then headed the remaining few blocks to Jena's house.

The kids were indeed surprised to see us back so soon. There was screaming and crying and hugging and where are our presents and on and on. Soon enough they realized Kendall was there. Leave it to Laney and Lissa to zero in on the prosthetic leg and go into question mode. They couldn't care less who he was, he was exciting, look mom he's missing a leg, that is so cool, can you take it off, and on and on. Lindy was the only one who bothered with asking a name, looking at the leg and saying gross. Sigh. Teenagers.

Finally, everyone calmed down and Jena appeared with tea for everyone.

"So do we have to leave already mom? We were planning a camping trip this weekend."

I was shocked to hear these words come from Lindy. Usually she was not the outdoors one of the family.

"Actually no you don't have to leave yet. I have some things I need to take care of at home and Jena has generously offered to let you stay for as long as it takes."

"Yay, are you finally kicking dad to the curb. He's such a dick."

"LINDY! Watch your mouth!"

"Why, it's true, he doesn't care about any of us. I don't know why you didn't throw him out years ago."

"Lindy, that is enough! I came home early and have things to take care of back home because of your father yes, but not why you think. You need to straighten up that attitude please."

She just glared at me then harrumphed and fell back on the sofa.

"Girls. Your father passed away couple of nights ago. I'm so sorry girls, he's gone."

Lindy looked a little shocked then shrugged. Laney and Lissa both looked at each other and started talking in their weird twin speak and started crying. Lissa joined me on my right side in the chair. Laney sat on the floor and put her head in my lap.

"We're sorry mommy. We didn't know he was sick. Do you have to clean the house is that why we are staying and your leaving again?"

That was one scenario I had never thought of. I was momentarily shocked speechless.

"Um, no. He wasn't sick."

"He was probably shot he was such a dick."

"Melinda Jameson! That is enough! What a terrible thing to say!"

"Why? He was a dick! You know how many times he called while we were here? The same number as when we are home, ZERO! He doesn't love or care about us. He's a creep and a jerk and could never spare even a minute to say good fricking night and I fricking love you to us! I'm glad he's dead! I hope he's in hell so at least you won't have to see him in heaven when you pass someday! He treated you worse than even us. You acted all nicey nice, but a dick is a dick mom. He wasn't nice to you! Who killed him huh? His mistress? Because I'm sure he had one!"

She stood up and ran from the room with tears streaming down her face.

Dear god. She was smarter than I had obviously given her credit for. How did she figure that all out? I had tears streaming too. I wasn't even sure how to console her. Should I stay with the twins or go to her?

Cera stood up then, "I'll go talk to her. Stay with the twins." I said a silent 'thank you Cera!'

They were both on the floor then holding each other.

I went over and sat with them. I put my arms around both of them and we all just sat and cried for a while.

"I don't want you to listen to that stuff your sister was saying girls. I know she is hurt, but your dad loved you. He was involved with some bad things at work though and it caught up with him. I don't know much more than that, I'm sorry. There is an investigation going on, and hopefully that will tell us more. But right now, I want you two to remember him in good ways. Find the happy memories and remember those. Ok?"

"OK mommy." Of course my Lissa would say that.

Laney though, a bit more like Lindy, said, "But mom, Lindy is right. He wasn't nice to you. We all saw that. I think you will be happier now." She leaned in to me to whisper, but was totally unsuccessful, "Like that Ken guy over there. He is HOT! I could stand him as a new dad."

What do you say to this? She thought she whispered, but that was far from what she did. Kendall actually got up and stepped out the front door. Jena dropped her cup and got up to go to the kitchen.

"Well Laney, yes, Kendall is very handsome. But your dad just passed away and that is not how I want you to think right now ok?"

"Well ok, but really, Dad may not have been dead, but he was gone long before now. I'm sad he's dead, but nothing really is going to change, he wasn't there before. Even when he was there, it's like he was a zombie. He just roamed round waiting for his next meal. It wasn't fun."

"Yeah Mom, that's true."

Well crap on a cracker, even the twins saw it. How the hell was I so ignorant to all of this.

Kendall and Jena had come back in at some point. Jena walked over and handed me a cup of tea.

"Would you girls like anything?"

Two no's were said in unison.

"Mommy? Can we go up to bed? I feel tired."

"Of course Lissa." I hugged them both to me. "Good night Lissa, Laney. I love you both so much!"

Truly

Jena got up then as well. "I think I will turn in as well. It sounds like we may have an early morning getting you off. It was nice to meet you Kendall. Goodnight Lena."

"I suppose I should go check on Lindy."

"Of course, in just a minute though, I want to hold you for a minute."

I went into his arms easily. It was safe, happy. And sad. This time tomorrow he would probably be gone.

"Hey you two. I think Lindy is ready to talk Lena."

"I will let you two be then. I have a room reserved at a hotel. I will be by to pick you up about 7:00." He leaned in then, "I love you Lena! Dream of me tonight!"

He kissed my cheek and left.

"Cera, how is she?"

"Pissed off. But I think she is just acting out in her shock and surprise. When she really realizes he is dead, I think she will be really upset."

"Yeah, I know. I'm so surprised at how much she had figured out though. How? Why? I don't know what to say to her."

"How about you listen, you may be surprised."

I hugged her then and went up to talk to my oldest daughter.

When I walked in the room she ran to my arms and started bawling.

"I'm sorry mommy, I'm sorry. I didn't mean to hurt you. I'm sorry dad died."

"Oh honey, I know, I'm sorry too. We will be ok though, I know we will."

"I know, mom, you're here. Why can't we go home with you? Why do we have to stay here now?"

"Well, there is still an investigation going on, and I really don't know what happened yet and what I may be going home to. I don't want to put you girls in a bad position. I think you will be safer here. As soon as I know what is going on there, I will bring you home. I promise I won't hold a funeral without you. But what I need from you is to be strong and kind for your sisters, ok?"

"I will mommy." She hugged me again and we sat on the bed until she fell asleep.

I went into the room Cera was in and laid down next to her and promptly fell asleep.

Cera woke me up early the next morning.

We had breakfast with the kids and promptly at 7 Kendall arrived.

"We have to go girls. I will call you every day, and you can call me too. I hope to be able to bring you home soon. I love you girls!"

I hugged them and we all cried a little more. I hoped I hadn't lied to them about getting them home soon. Surely the cops had some idea what had happened and things would be normal soon.

Chapter 25

Getting to the airport was not a problem. Since we were on a private carrier, not leaving the country and had already dealt with customs, we were able to drive directly to where the plane was stored. We boarded without any issues from the press. We took off about an hour later.

Cera went to the front of the plane and plugged in so to give us a bit of privacy.

"I know I shouldn't be sad about you not staying, but I am. I wish you could stay."

"I know, I do too. I'm going directly home though and getting my work concerns dealt with and I plan to come back soon to help you out. Surely the police have some idea what happened and the brokerage company and lawyers will be dealing with the scandal. We'll be together soon I promise, soon."

"I know. Thank you Kendall. What do you think will happen when we arrive? Will it be a crazy as yesterday?"

"Probably. I won't lie. But I do have security lined up and an attorney on retainer for you. Cera retained one as well. They are going to meet us at the airport. They will actually come to the plane and you will leave directly form the plane. You should not have any problems until you get home. The important thing is to let your attorneys and security do their jobs and you do what they say ok?"

"OK. I will, I certainly don't know how to deal with media shit storms."

"Well, the people I hired do. They all come very highly recommended."

"I'm certain I can pay for them; why didn't you tell me before you retained them?"

Jill Edick

"Well judging by the card situation you were having in Thailand, plus the amount of problems that are sure to come up because of the scandal, I would not be surprised if there was no money for you to do anything with. At least not right away. Your assets have been frozen. But, if that is not the case, then by all means, send me a check. Otherwise, please accept this until such a time as you get through the rest of this chaos. We can set up a payback when this is all done ok?"

"Fair enough. But I really can't imagine I won't have access to my own money. That seems Ludacris."

"You can't imagine how much I hope you are right. But enough of that. I don't have much time with you, let's talk about anything else."

We spent the rest of the trip talking about the trip, the girls, each other, our future. The trip went way to fast. All to soon the pilot was announcing our decent.

Once we landed, the plane was directed to a private hangar to refuel and unload its passengers. We were greeted by our attorney's; to my surprise both were women. And a security team, once again headed up by a woman. There was certainly muscle in the form of men, but the ones in charge were all women. That was nice. Other than Kendall, I wasn't sure I wanted to deal with men right now.

I really liked my attorney right away. She was sharp and straight forward.

"I'm Patricia Moore. You must be Darlena. And this is your mess. First, my condolences on the death of your husband. Second, I want you to remove all things 'worry' right now. That is my job. If you listen to me, I will get you through this. I won't promise it will be easy, but we will prevail. When you inevitably start worrying, call me. Third, once we leave this plane, you speak to no one, look at no one, comment to no one. I will be your voice until we are in a secure place. I have already worked with security and we have a safe house established for you should things at your house go as I expect they may. It is right now I am going to refer you back to the second rule, you do not worry. I know you have a million questions, and I will certainly address what I can as quickly as I can but this is neither the time nor place, ok?"

It looked like Cera was getting a similar discussion. I wondered what on earth for, she hadn't been married to Geoff. But I suppose guilt by association would be the press point of view.

"Hi Darlena! I'm Tamela. I own and run the security company that has been hired for your protection. These brutes with me are Jose, Justin and Tiny Tim. They will be your personal guard from this point forward. They will be rotating shifts. I will go over all of that with you once we get you settled. For now, we will be escorted by all three."

Cera was back with me. She looked a bit freaked out. I hope there wouldn't be any repercussions for her.

"Hey, I'm good. I need an attorney simply for talking to the police about my investigation. It's all good. You about ready? You want me to escort these fine folks out so you can have your goodbye?"

"Thanks Cera!"

Everyone started piling off the plane with arm loads of bags and got into cars waiting by the plane.

Before I could say a thing I was in Kendall's arms with the most sensuous kiss being planted square on my lips. I never wanted that to stop, but all to quickly he pulled back.

"Lena, my Lena. I don't want you to leave. I want to just take you away from all of this, make you mine forever. Dammit this was harder than I thought."

"Kendall."

"My love."

We kissed again. I was crying and Kendall was certainly trying hard to hold back tears.

I turned and left, I knew if I didn't I never would. I bolted down the stairs and didn't look back until I was in a car with Tiny Tim, and Patricia.

I looked up the stairs and he was standing there staring. Then he turned his back to me and pointed at his rear end, gave a thumbs up turned his head and smiled then walked back on the plane. I burst out laughing. Oh how I loved that ass, I was so glad that the man with it was such a pure gem. My heart swelled with love for him.

The cars started to pull away and Patricia jumped on what to expect when we arrived at the house.

"The media was already camped out when we went by earlier. We are going to park in the driveway as close to the house as possible. Tim will get out first and open the door for you. Once you are out he will take you immediately inside. Please have your keys ready. I will go to the media and give them a simple statement. I'm going to tell them you have just returned from a very long trip and need peace. At this time, we do not know anything about the investigation and therefore have no comment. I will leave them at that point. Megan, Cera's attorney, has already made arrangements for the police to come over later today to fill you in with what they can and to get Cera's statement. Once we know what is going on, we will decide if it is best for you to stay at your house or if we should move you a safe house."

She stopped talking, then grabbed my hand. "Hey, it's ok. It's going to work out. remember? Megan and I work in the same firm; you will both be well represented. We are very good at our jobs. Trust us please?"

"Of Course. I just don't understand. But I guess I will in time right?"

"Well, most things yes, truth has a way of being found in these situations. Whether or not you understand what your husband was thinking and doing, well I can't promise that."

"Thank you for your honesty."

Right then we turned the corner towards my house and what a scene awaited us. There were media vans everywhere. People all over the street, cameras aimed our way. It was a total zoo. I turned away from the window and dug into my purse for keys to be ready to bolt. Patricia squeezed my hand and said "show time!"

Chapter 26

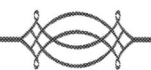

The whole car to house thing actually went just as Patricia said it would. What a scene though. My neighbors must be having a complete fit. I made a mental note to plan a huge block party once this was all over to thank them for their support.

Cera, her lawyer and another body guard were behind us, and the last car with Tamela and the final body guard and a few pieces of luggage, well, alright, all of it, were right behind them. Patricia's statement to the press was very quick and soon we were all in the house sitting around my table. Security had already been through the place. All windows and doors locked.

Tamela announced that I need new door locks all around and cameras indoors and out. I couldn't believe all that was necessary and said so.

She looked right at me, but spoke to my attorney, "Is she this naïve or that uninformed? What does she think is going on here? Her husband was murdered, details not yet released, but my sources say it was not a pretty death, the murderer is still out there, there is a billion-dollar scandal that her husband was more than likely responsible for, if not responsible, then at the very least up to his eyebrows in, and she thinks she doesn't need better door locks?" She stopped staring at me and turned to Patricia, "I'm going to go get things moving while you explain to your client that I was paid extremely handsomely to make sure she stays alive and well." She turned back to me. "I am hoping that no one has filled you in on the magnitude of the situation you are in and that is why you are being so blasé, but you need to catch up quick. This is not going to be the best time of your life. I am not trying to be a bitch, but I won't waste my time or my client's money on someone who doesn't care. I will help you, I will be your best friend in this, but you have to listen and not question me. OK?"

I just shook my head. What didn't I know, what the hell was going on? I wasn't worried so much as furious that I obviously was the most ignorant person in the room to the problems here.

"Of course I will listen, I'm not stupid or some condescending rich bitch. I just have no idea what is going on. I went on a trip with my best friend, I left married, with a nice home, and a fair savings account. I got a call that shortened my trip that I am now a widow, my money has been inaccessible since I left on the trip, and now I have you yelling at me in MY dining room telling me my husband was murdered in a not pretty manner and stole billions of dollars! I think someone needs to start telling me what the hell is going on! For the love of god, I am a housewife in the suburbs who works part time in a doctor's office doing transcription, raising three girls and two dogs! That is what I know, so someone, and I don't' care who, NEEDS TO SATRT TALKING!"

The only one not staring at me completely wide eyed and shocked was Cera. She came over and stood beside me, I didn't even realize I had stood up. She held my hand and looked at everyone.

"This is the sweetest person I know. She is not stupid, she is not naïve, and she DOES NOT deserve to be spoken to like she is. She is a happy, positive person who has spent the last 15 years being a faithful wife and an outstanding mother. She has taken care of her children and home. The only thing she has done wrong was tangle with and then marry that pile of excrement that was Geoff. He controlled her, the money, the bills, the household. She had no reason to question him, she trusted him for fucks sake! You know trust, it is something some people do, it's that thing you all have been asking her and I to do with you, TRUST! Now I am here to assist the police in their investigations both with the death of her husband, and lets loose the 'murder' word, it's crass, and the potential trading mess. My friend here will help you completely, I know her and I will not allow anyone here to make her feel guilty of anything but being a loving and trusting human being who yes, made mistakes, who here hasn't, but is NOT RESPONSILE FOR SOME JACKWAGONS IDIOT SCREWUPS! You may be security, and tiny Tim, may be the largest human I have ever met in my life, but I am Lena's Pitbull. I will love you and snuggle you and be a great friend and companion, until you threaten my human! Then I will eat you alive! I will protect Lena or I will die trying! If I die trying though, I promise I will take with me the assholes trying to hurt Lena! Are we clear on who is who now and how we will behave while in this home?"

Again, a stunned silence and a lot of open mouth stares were across the room.

Patricia was the first to break the silence, "Where have you been all my life? Do you need a job? I have one for you if you ever need one. This has just become my favorite all time case and I haven't done much yet. Megan, how did we get these two? This is a dream come true! We are going to kick ass all over this city! I will be the first to apologize. We came into this not knowing what you know or don't. We also don't know much because the cops have been so tight lipped. But I, for one, am here to help you Darlena, and I will be Pitbull number two if you will let me. But I too am not going to lie to you, this is a giant mess that we don't even know the whole story about. This isn't going to be easy." She turned to Tamela. "For the time being, run any security concerns through myself or my assistant at the office. I agree we need to tighten down the house here. But I think more importantly, we need to get you someplace else Darlena. This is not going to be a good place for you to stay. Unfortunately, this will only get worse before it gets better."

"I don't want to leave my home. My neighbors are friends, I love it here. Why do you think I should leave it?"

"Honey, I promise you this, your neighbors may have been friends in the past, but some serious crap is going to go down. You are about to find out who your friends really are, and I will bet you the cost of my service that your neighbors will not be your friends til the end. I'm sorry."

"What happened? Can someone please tell me what is going on now?"

"I will be happy to. But, I don't know much yet. Megan? Are the files on their way over?"

"Yes they are, and the police will be here around 4 this afternoon."

"So we haven't seen the actual paperwork on either investigation yet Darlena, we really are blind right now too. We know only what has been reported in the news and what Tamela has been able to find out through connections in the police department. I hate to tell you things that just aren't accurate. Can you wait until the police are done interviewing Cera and we have had a chance to review the case files?"

"I suppose. Do I really have a choice?"

Tamela stepped up then. "I'm sorry my behavior was so offensive. I have many excuses and stories I could tell you about lying clients, but I believe you are not one of those. I just needed to know who I was working with so I know how best to protect you. That being said, I agree with Ms. Moore completely. I think we need to get you out of here. I need to lock down this house and get you someplace where you will be both comfortable and safe while this is going on. I think it would be best if you and Cera started packing up some things while we wait for the police to arrive."

"What things?"

"Everything you cherish. Get your photos, personal items you can't live without. Any financial documents you know about. Clothing for you and the kids. We don't have a lot of space to move things, but we can get the things that are personal to you, things you don't want to see taken away from you if the government should decide to seize the property."

"Also, we need to address your money. My understanding is that any account with Geoff's name on them have been frozen already. If you have any accounts without his name on them, we need to liquidate that money as soon as possible."

"Well I do have a couple of account is just my name. I can transfer the money to Cera. The girls have savings accounts too. But Geoff's name may be on those, I'm not sure."

Truly

"Let's take a look. If he is not on the accounts, let's get it all transferred right away. We can take Cera to the bank in the morning to get that cash for you."

So started a miserable afternoon of transferring a pittance of money that I was supposed to be able to live on indefinitely, and picking and choosing what the girls and I couldn't live without and watching it all get packed away into three cars. That's all, three cars for my whole life. And those three cars still had to hold us people too.

Cera got to escape once to go to the bank. She said it was crazy. I believe I heard her say something about Geoff and being and eternal dick even hell didn't want. At this point I was done arguing with that too.

At 3:45 the police arrived. They spent over an hour with Cera. Her attorney agreed to go with them to pick up copies of the investigation stuff after they were done.

Then it was my turn.

They wanted to know about the 'large' withdrawal I made before leaving on my trip. "Large? $1500 is large? OK, I used much of it on the trip because my credit card wasn't working. I have all my receipts and what is left of it in my wallet, would you like to see them?"

They did. So I brought it all along with my transaction register. They all looked at me including my lawyer like they couldn't believe it. "What? I'm a bit of a perfectionist about my money. I like to know where it all is. I can honestly say now that I wish I was more involved in the household money since that bastard wiped us out! But I wasn't and now I have about $37.00 to my name."

The detective working on the murder end said he was good and another detective investigating the money part said at this point they had what they needed.

"My client would like to be filled in on what is going on then since there does not seem to be any reason to suspect her of anything."

"We brought a synopsis for you as requested. Since these are two active investigations and your client is not a suspect, we cannot divulge details at this time. You understand of course counselor."

"Of course. My client certainly has a right to know what is going on however."

"Understood. More detail than she will probably ever want is in the synopsis, we can go over it, we thought perhaps you would want to do it though. There is some information about a few attorneys that the deceased had. They told us earlier that they will be contacting you to set up meeting with Mrs. Jameson as well. Their information is in the file as are cards should your client have any questions or think of something that could be useful."

Patricia sat down after letting the officers out and started reading. She threw one file aside pretty quickly. The other file took her longer. After reading it she tossed it aside with a mumble comment I didn't catch then opened an envelope, picked up her phone and started giving information to someone and told them to call her when the meetings were scheduled. After she hung up she turned to me and Cera and Megan who had joined me.

"Well folks, this is a tale that frankly has me disgusted on many levels." She handed the smaller file to Megan who opened it started reading and much like Patricia tossed it aside pretty quickly.

"That is the synopsis of the murder investigation. Nothing real interesting in here other that a few details the public don't have. I'm not going to share them, frankly it is disturbing. I will tell you this, Geoff was certainly murdered and quite viciously. The police are looking for a team. Specifically, a woman that he was apparently living with whom they have discovered was married. It would seem that this couple disappeared right after the murder. The motive seems to be money, like many other people this couples lifesaving was invested with Geoff and went down the crapper. The police don't believe that they're a threat to you or your kids Darlena, however, I will feel better when you are safely relocated."

"How did he die? Was it quick? I mean he may have been the world's biggest bastard, but that doesn't mean he should have suffered."

Patricia and Megan looked at each other. Then Patricia looked at Cera then me. "I told you I wouldn't lie to you Darlena. Do you really want that question answered?"

Cera grabbed my hand and squeezed. "Yes. I want to try to understand why this all happened."

"Well the nature of the death was rather vindictive, cruel. It looks more like a revenge from a woman scorned. However, the strength that would have been required to pull off what happened indicates either a very very strong woman or a man had to be involved. They know that their prime suspect was not a big or strong woman, her husband however is. He also has a criminal record as such has had a hard time finding work. She is the bread winner, and every dime they didn't need to live she squirreled away. She worked for the same company as Geoff which is likely how they met. When he was hot with the stock, it looks as though she cozied up to him knowing his reputation as a womanizer. Apparently she thought she could get rich quick if she took up with him. Not sure how the husband felt about that, I would guess that judging by the viciousness of the attack, neither of them were happy with the relationship."

"What did they do?"

"I'm not going to give you the details, frankly, I need a drink to try and erase that from my brain, but suffice it to say, if Geoff had actually survived that, he would never have cheated on you again."

"Cripes! I knew he was a pig, but damn." It was a rare day to see Cera have nothing further to say. The images running in my head were nauseating, I was glad that my attorney did not think I needed to see or hear more.

"Um, OK. So the second folder?"

Megan was still reading on that one. She looked more disgusted if possible with that one than the first.

"Megan is our financial crimes specialist; I think I will let her explain that convoluted mess."

"Well, convoluted mess is right. This investigation is still ongoing, and they suspect that at least two other people are involved. The losses at this point are in the upper millions, bordering on a billion. That is a lot of money. The interesting thing is, that much of that was not in stocks. They aren't sure where the money went and they aren't sure who else is involved. They have suspects, but can't find a paper trail. This was good. These creeps covered their trail good. This had to have been going on for years. You just don't see the record breaking numbers that Geoff was having and then every single dime just disappears overnight. There were four other broker having a great couple of years, but two of them they think just jumped on Geoff's coattails and followed him like little puppies. They lost everything and there is a paper trail on them. The other two though, nothing, there is just nothing. They were smarter than Geoff. He came onto the radar because of his lavish lifestyle. He got a taste of money and flaunted it. These other two not so much. The detectives aren't sure yet if Geoff was an arrogant ring leader or an unsuspecting patsy. I feel for the ones who have to attempt to sort this out. This is a disaster. The only one right now they can conclusively tie to anything was Geoff. This investigation could go on for years, and even then we may never know what the hell happened. I'm glad I didn't have my money with these jerks. In the meantime, thousands of people did and have lost every single dime. There are a lot of angry people. It makes me wonder how the police narrowed down their murder investigation so quickly. Frankly, I don' think you need to worry about Geoff's accused assailants as much as you need to worry about the pissed off many that lost their retirements in this."

Tamela entered the room then. "Ladies, I am sorry to interrupt, but I think we need to get moving. There are crowds growing out front that are much more than media. I contacted the police and they are trying to control the crowds, but that is not a happy group out there."

When we had packed earlier, the cars had been pulled onto the yard in the back so to be out of the line of sight of the media. They were still out back thankfully. There was now another larger SUV back there with heavily tinted windows. Tiny Tim was standing next to that one and a window was down and my baby puppies were looking out.

"Babies! You got my puppies!"

"Yes, when I sent Tim to get the other car, I had him pick up your girls too. No need for them to become victims in this too. I got the larger car to offer better protection for you ladies. Plus, we loaded a few more things for you in the cars and there really wasn't room for people. So if everyone is ready, I think now would be an excellent time to leave."

We climbed into the SUV and slowly started making our way up the driveway. The crowd was out of control. It took forever to get past all the people and media. As I looked at my neighbor's windows as we drove by many were standing there glaring a few even flipped us off. It was an absolute mob scene. It took forever just to get out of the neighborhood. Then we had cars following us and media following. It was absolutely insane. We drove around for over an hour before the security detail decided we had lost the crowds. I don't know how that was possible, but I trusted they did. We ended up in another suburb of Philly. Not a real great one, but I couldn't complain either. We pulled into a parking garage that required parking permits to enter. We parked at the end and headed up an elevator to the top floor. We had an apartment towards the backside of the building, so we were looking at the back of another building from our window, but would not see or be seen from the front. It wasn't beautiful, but comfortable and clean. I was so exhausted that I just wanted to fall asleep. I called the girls to see how they were holding up and then went to bed.

Chapter 27

Across the World:

He had just arrived at his home and was standing in his bedroom. Her scent was still in the air. He walked to the bed and breathed in her scent from the pillow she had slept on. Her scent was intoxicating. He vowed right then, he was never washing that pillow case again. He curled up in bed with his face buried in the pillow and cried.

Patricia and Megan both returned in the morning. They were both going with me to meetings with two other attorneys today. Patricia had managed to get in contact with the two that Geoff had hired and made appointments. One it turned out was the attorney he had draw up a will. The other was one he had hired to take care of financial documents and he had used in his large purchases to take care of the money.

"I hope you don't mind Darlena, I thought I would bring Megan along, she is already up to speed in your situation and she is our firms money person, I told you that yesterday right? Anyway, I thought she should be there to help us through some of the finer details."

"You did mention that she was the financial guru. What is your specialty?"

"I specialize in criminal law, specifically though, I typically work with spouses and family of those who get caught up in white collar crimes, much like what you're in right now. I help the families to deal with the unfortunate consequences of the crime committed by their family or friends that they got drug into knowingly or unknowingly."

"Are you busy? I wouldn't' think there would be that much for you to do."

"Oh, white collar crimes are huge! Unless it's monumental and something else happens like example, with Geoff, most white collar crimes are ignored by the media and public in general. People are worried about murders, rapes, B&E. Stock fraud they don't care about. They don't think it's dangerous. At least not until it affects their retirement. Then they get ticked off. Unfortunately, it's people like you who had no idea what your spouse was doing that take enormous hits. It's not right, and that is where I come in. I do some defense cases, I do some seizure cases, I do a lot of divorces. I work a lot with Megan and a couple of other attorneys in our practice to get the details I need to proceed with my cases. We all work together. We are one firm with different specialties. We are good. We are also all female. That doesn't mean we don't work with male clients, but we find that so many women want other women to help them. When you're going through something like this, it's nice to have another woman on your side."

"Wow. I'm impressed. And I'm glad you're my attorney."

"Thank you. Now, our appointment is at 10:00. Both attorneys have agreed to meet together at our offices downtown. So we should get going. Cera is of course welcome to come as well, that is entirely up to you."

"Yes, I would like her to come along if she wants. Cera?!"

She was still in her room, I wasn't even sure she was up yet, but she buzzed right out the door when I called though, dressed and ready. "I heard everything. Let's go!"

Nothing is sacred when you live with your best friend.

Cera and I rode with one of our security guys in the SUV. I think it was with Justin, but maybe it was Jose. I wasn't sure of anything other than it wasn't Tim or Tamela. We met Patricia and Megan at their office building. We had been given a parking pass to their garage. I didn't see any media, but I felt better knowing we were in a secure area.

Patricia took us straight to a conference room. We were sitting down and getting coffee when the other attorneys arrived. They introduced themselves as Jackson Smythe and Darien Logan. I had a hard time believing they were either one attorneys, they both looked about 12.

Mr. Smythe was the 'will' guy apparently. He took the reins; said he would start with the good news in this whole fiasco. Not very professional in my opinion, but I guess what do you expect from a guy so wet behind the ears, he probably still met with his frat brothers on the weekends for beer pong. No wonder Geoff hired these two. He could easily control them and no doubt they were cheap and eager for a high roller client.

He read the will. It really was mostly what I expected. The house would go to myself as would the cars and our bank accounts. There was a bank account that was in Geoff's and another woman's name, she was the beneficiary to that one. There were three life insurance policies, I only knew of one. Two of them I was the beneficiary on, the other was named to the same woman I had no idea who she was. There was also a funeral fund and last wishes drawn up and paid for. Except for the unknown woman, it seemed pretty cut and dried.

Mr. personality said he was done and turned it over to the other attorney. He was at least a little friendlier and offered condolences before he started in.

"I took care of the large dollar contracts, finances etc. My office acts like something of a trust, you set up your large purchase and contracted bills with us, we pay them from your "trust". We read contracts before they are signed and negotiate terms and process payments when our clients would prefer not to deal with them or prefer to remain anonymous in a deal. I'm afraid I am not going to be the bearer of any good news today."

He pulled out an enormous file. He also had one for me and one for Patricia so we could follow along. Patricia handed the file to Megan who immediately started scanning it. Her expression said a lot. I sighed. What could he possibly say that was worse than what the police said yesterday?

Oh how I wish I hadn't had that thought.

Truly

"First I will state; your husband was significantly behind in payments to his account with us so we could pay his bills. When contacted he said do what we can and he would catch up eventually. Well I'm sure you can imagine that was not a real positive response with his creditors. With regards to the house in Flourtown, it is in a state of foreclosure. We have only been able to make tiny payments for about six months, then five months ago we were unable to make any payments. We have done the best we can to prevent the foreclosure, but we were served the final paperwork just two weeks ago. You have to be out by the end of the month or they will lock you out. I shared this with Geoff, he said let them have the dump, I do believe that was a direct quote before he hung up on me. I sent him a certified letter explaining that this will destroy not just his credit, but yours as well and that the mortgage company can come after both of you for losses incurred. He did sign for the letter, there is a copy of it here, but he never responded."

There was much paper shuffling then he continued.

"With regard to the Jeep Cherokee, and the Lexus, both are financed, both have not been paid for six months nor has the insurance on them. The finance companies have been trying to repo them for over a month but have been unable to locate them. Additionally, there is an issue with a Jaguar. Your name is not on that one though, it is in Geoff's name and that other woman mentioned in the will. If you know the location of any of these vehicles though it would be in your best interest to let me know so I can notify the companies to come collect them. Otherwise you will potentially be sued. In addition, if they cannot recover the amount you owe when they sell these vehicles, you will be responsible for the difference with the exception of the Jaguar."

WHAT??? My mind was reeling! I thought my car was paid off. It was five years old for crying out loud. Before I could speak these thoughts he continued.

"I am sorry to report in regards to the insurance policies and funeral policy, they have all lapsed. They were canceled by the insurance providers after failure to pay about nine months ago. There are no life insurance policies I am aware of to draw on. There is also no funeral policy. Any final arrangements you need to make will be yours to pay. This brings me to the bank accounts. The account with us is empty. Our fee has not been paid for four months and no funds have been deposited with which to pay the bills we were contracted to take care of. My firm has already started the process of collecting on the fees we are due. At this time all assets we could possibly put a lien on have either been frozen by the federal government, or are in a state of collection themselves. There are approximately ten credit cards all maxed out and no payments made. Again that we are aware of. I cannot share with you anything that he did not share with us. So there could be more debt I don't know of. The only other item in question with our firm is the penthouse in Manhattan. That is also in a state of foreclosure. However, that is not your concern as it was in Geoff's and the other woman's name."

I was freaking out. I couldn't even catch my breath much less respond. Megan did though.

"What about Life insurance, retirement benefits and medical policies through Geoff's work, or any mention of college funds for the children. I don't see any mention of them here, did you try to put a lien on any of those things or look into possible benefit payouts there?"

"What we could find was nothing. I can comfortably tell you there are absolutely no assets. We have done a very thorough asset search and found absolutely nothing in Geoff's name. We cannot go after your client's assets in her name only, not that those are much, as she was not under contract with us. I can also say, there are more debts out there. Some in your client's name, many not. As a courtesy I included a copy of the asset search and liability findings for you to pursue. I will also let you know; our firm is planning to place an asset lien on the estate in the event that any money comes out of it that the government doesn't take."

He turned to me. He must have seen the shock on my face, or perhaps it was the tears streaming down my face, but he softened a bit. "I am sorry Mrs. Jameson. It would appear you are surprised by what I am telling you and I really hate being the bearer of this news. Your husband was not a good man, he hurt a lot of people. But at the end of the day, none more than you and your kids. He has left you a terrible legacy and I am genuinely sorry for what you are about to go through."

He turned to Patricia who had been taking notes fast and furious.

"If I can be of any further assistance, please call me. At the end of the day we don't want to hurt your client further. I have included the information to contact the car collectors if your client knows where the cars can be found, or you can contact me with that information and I will handle it. Thank you all for your time."

The two attorneys got up and left without further comment.

I held it together until they left, then I ran to the nearest trash can and threw up. I then fell over onto the floor and started bawling like and infant without their teddy bear. I was laying there crying when I felt Cera lie down behind me and hold me. She didn't say anything, just held me until I finally stopped crying. I have no idea how long I had been like that. I finally came back to my senses and started to sit up. Cera got up and helped me. All the blinds in the conference room had been drawn, and there was a pitcher of water and a box of tissues on the table as well as a warm towel and a pack of gum. I looked at Patricia. She just smiled sadly and looked back at her file.

Cera helped me over to a chair. I blew my nose, used the towel to wipe my hands and face, then popped a piece of gum. I said a silent prayer of thanks to Kendall for finding me the perfect attorney.

After I got myself a little more together I turned to Patricia for advice.

"Okay. So not great news there, but I think we can handle this." She looked to Megan for confirmation.

"Yes, this is something we can handle. We have also done our own asset search as well as debt search. The report he provided is accurate. There are no assets, I'm afraid, for you or the girls. There is a lot of debt too. But we can take care of that. Nothing there that can't be handled, we just have to move quickly. While we still have access to the house and belongings, we need to clear it out and liquidate things. It's going to be seized before foreclosure can happen, so we might as well get the assets while we can. We can have her pay them to us for attorney fees. When this is all said and done, we can then issue a refund. She may stand a chance at getting something back with us. Nothing if we let it all go."

"OK, get started."

Megan left then and Patricia turned back to me.

"OK, so your husband is dead. You can't really divorce him. Unfortunate. The creditors are going to come for you; we will take care of that. But we don't want them to come after you for things that aren't your problem just because you were married to him, and they will try to come after you if they can't find this other woman. Your credit is shot. You will recover, but it will take a long time. You are about to have repossession, foreclosure and soon bankruptcy on your credit. But again, you will recover from those things. We need to locate those cars for the finance companies as well, those may have value, in which case we will sell them and pay the debt so you can keep the equity. If they are upside down, we will let the creditors repo them and include the balances due in the bankruptcy. We need to find out right away though, we need to file your bankruptcy as soon as possible. The sooner we separate you from Geoff and the debt, the better. I'm afraid this is just the tip of the iceberg and we need to cut the head off this dragon. We need to strike quickly."

"What about 'the other woman' should we let the police know the information we learned today?"

"I already sent my assistant a message to let the cops know about this woman. If she is the one, they are suspecting they need to know this information. Everything else that will come, will be personal lawsuits. We are talking about a massive amount of money that your husband stole. Since there is not yet anyone else to blame, I promise, people who lost money will come after the only person they can, Geoff's estate. In other words, you. We need to start protecting you and your children immediately from this. We have got to separate you any way possible,

Truly

we need to show your loss too. We need to show the kids loss. We need to make it impossible for you to pay for his crap. I can't stop the lawsuits from coming, but I can prevent them from leaving you unable to live. I would also like you to think about changing your name."

"Changing my name? Why?"

"Well, it won't get you away from lawsuits and the credit. But it will give you a fresh start should you decide to move away from the area. You are going to be recognizable for a while, but with your current last name, you will be memorable for a long long time. If you stay in the area you're going to struggle either way. But if you move you will be able to start over easier. Think about how you will find jobs, rent someplace to live, with Jameson you will not get any of those things for a long time. With say your maiden name, you will at least be given a chance. Your kids are going to be a different issue. You can file for name changes, but that will cause more backlash I think than just letting it go. If you move, they will recover pretty quickly, kids won't know or care about their last name and parents will be more in tune to you than them. It isn't going to cure everything, but you changing your name may make them a little easier. We can get the name change paperwork processing as soon as the bankruptcy is filed."

I was so overwhelmed. I was starting to shut down. I knew I was not thinking of something, but I didn't know what.

Cera was the one to ask the questions I couldn't.

"What about funeral expenses and medical insurance. I am pretty sure Geoff carried the insurance for the family, is that still intact and will Lena be able to get Cobra?"

"Well, I will have to look into the medical insurance, but I'm pretty sure based on what I looked at in that file, all insurance and retirement bene's Geoff may have opted for he canceled long ago to get more money in his paycheck. I will send a request to his employer for information and let you know. The funeral is a different story. You have no means with which to pay for this. You can apply for victim's assistance, but that could take forever to get and may not cover the expenses. So please don't take this wrong, but your other option would be to not claim his body. The medical examiner will contact the next of kin. In this case you. If you do not respond to collect his remains, they will try to locate another family member. If say a parent or sibling claims his remains, then the expenses become theirs. If no next of kin comes forward or is found, then the state will cremate and dispose of the remains. I know that isn't a great option, and it may make you feel bad, but I want you to think about what he said about your home. Think about the financial situation he left you in. Think about the damage he has created for your children. Is he worth more debt to give him a nice funeral that will probably be protested? If he has any other family, you can give me their info and I will pass it on to the state, and then I would walk away. You have to make that decision though."

If there was anything in my stomach, I am sure I would have thrown up again.

"I think Lena has had enough for one day. I think maybe I should take her home to get some rest."

"I agree. Here is a short list of things I need some answers for by say tomorrow morning. You rest Darlena, then talk these things over with Cera and make some decisions and see if you can provide some answers to questions. Ok?"

I shook my head.

"You two hang here for a minute. I'm going to get security for you so you can get back to the apartment." She handed Cera the paper and left the room.

I really don't remember much after that. We left the office, drove to the apartment, and I was put to bed.

Chapter 28

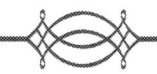

Across the World:

"Are you sure this is what you want to do son?"

"Yes, I can't live without her. I'm not quitting on you, just moving my part of the operation overseas."

"I certainly understand loving a woman. We raised you well son. You know I will do whatever it takes to make this happen for you."

A month later:

Why hadn't he heard from her? He had called, left messages, texted and called again. Was she all right? Were they alright? He couldn't wait any longer, he needed her!

I felt like the worst mom on the planet. Possibly the worst human on the planet. I couldn't function. I couldn't eat, I slept for crap, I called my job and they invited me to not return. If it weren't for Cera I don't know how I would have survived the next month.

She had got car info to the attorneys. She helped her attorney get my household packed, moved to storage and anything worth anything sold. She gave them the name of Geoffs family members to deal with the remains. She even talked with the girls and explained the situation to them. They were sad they couldn't attend a funeral, but weren't pitching fits. She arranged for some counseling for the girls and got us all set up on state funded medical insurance so we at least had something. She convinced me changing my name was good and filled out paper work for me. She was my rock. She took me to a counselor too and slowly I started to return to myself.

Patricia was right, lawsuits started coming down. I had court dates for my name change and bankruptcy. She took care of the other lawsuits. The police were looking for the mystery woman and her husband. It seemed that they had disappeared out of the country and there was no sign of them anywhere. The police did not think I was in danger from them at any rate.

Finally, after a month Cera said it was time to move on. The girls needed me closer to them, and I needed to get away from Pennsylvania. Most of the belongings I had taken from the house Cera had already had shipped to her place in Colorado.

"Where am I supposed to go? I have no job, I can't afford anything. I know the girls can't stay with your sister forever, but what am I supposed to do?"

"You are supposed to live Lena! You are better than this! Your girls need you! You need them! You need to get your life back! Yes, it's going to be hard. Yes, it's going to be different. But you can't stay holed up in this shitty apartment forever. You have adult responsibilities and things you need to deal with! I need to get my office set up at home. I have my own life to live. I love you, I will do anything for you, but I won't die here and I won't let you! My neighbors in Broomfield, the ones who watch my place while I'm gone, they decided to move. I bought their place. I am going to be a landlord. And I have no tenants. Let's go home, let's go back to Colorado. You and the girls can be my tenants. I will work with you while you find a job. It's time Lena! And while I'm throwing down, have you even noticed what was delivered the other day? Have you forgotten Thailand and everything in it?"

Shit, shit Damn! What had I become? My girls, how could I have been such a horrible mother! Cera, my god how have I abused our friendship. My love, how had I forsaken that? I haven't touched my phone in weeks. I wasn't even sure it was charged or where the charger was. Cera had been calling the girls and putting me on her phone. I hadn't notice much in this apartment. Things have come in almost daily as the storage unit has been sorted and things sold. So I looked where Cera had pointed and there were three boxes from Thailand. Our wine, Kendall had sent the wine. He hadn't forgotten me, how had I been so negligent of him?

"Oh my gawd Cera! What the hell have I become? I need to go to my kids. I need to go. I'm drowning here, there is nothing here I love. Why am I here? When can we leave?"

"There's my girl! I will get a truck rented and start getting crap packed up. We can drive to Colorado, it will be a real road trip! Yay! We're going home!"

She went into hyper drive and I found my phone charger and called my girls and told them I was coming home and we had a place to live. They were so excited and so was I. I started feeling better and better. I was getting excited again. I called Patricia to let her know my plans. She told me what I needed to do so she could continue to represent me. There would be of course a book of paperwork to assign her as my representative in court and to deal with all the nonsense that had come up. Finally, I called Kendall. I didn't even know what time it was there. But he answered.

"Love! My love is that you? I have been calling and calling, please tell me your all right!"

I couldn't help it, I started laughing.

"Music to my ears. Oh Lena, are you ok? I have been so worried."

"I'm ok. Getting better. I guess I kind of snapped for a while. But it's getting better. I'm getting better."

We talked for a while, I told him of the plans to move.

He told me about the farm and the new venture his mom was doing. She had so much fun teaching me to cook and writing up recipes for me, she decided to open a tourist cooking class shop in Chaing Mai and she wrote a cook book!

I had missed his voice, it was so wonderful to hear it. But I wished he was here. I missed him so much. After we hung up, I immediately got a text message. It was a picture from Kendall...of his ass. I made it my wallpaper. Then went about packing the mess that was the apartment.

Cera and I got things squared away in about a week and we were packed and ready to be on the road only five days after my awakening. The morning we were preparing to leave, we went out and in addition to the U-Haul, there was a trailer behind it with a small truck on it.

"LU-LU TRUCK! Cera, why is she here?"

"Well, when Megan and I were going through things for liquidation I found your old truck in the garage. We went through all the financial files and found the title. It's in your name. Only your name. Your maiden name. No liens. So I got in it and found the key in the glove box with all your maintenance records. Did Geoff know you still took care of this truck and, if I know you, drove it? Anyway, It's yours. It cannot be touched by anyone with regards to Geoff. You have a car. I couldn't leave that behind. So I put it in storage before the government took the house."

"I can keep Lulu? I didn't think I would be able too. Are you sure?"

"Yup, Megan and Patricia gave it their blessing. It's yours, never was his. So now you have your little truck back. It's kind of like you and that cell phone plan of yours. You never did cave on that either did you!"

She busted up laughing. It was true, I refused to give up my old truck or my cell phone plan when I married Geoff. He had a fit, but I held my ground. Right now I was glad I had. When I went to college, my parents refused to get me a car or a cell phone. So I took all my savings from babysitting, and bought the little truck and my own cell phone plan. I pre-paid for a full year of service and every year after I paid for a full year so I wouldn't have monthly bills. I loved the freedom it gave me and I flat refused to let those two things go. Once Geoff started making money though he insisted on a better car to drive his children around in. I agreed to a bigger car, but refused to sell my truck. It was a source of many arguments.

"Nope, I never caved. Between Geoff and my parents, they hated that truck. Too bad!"

We both laughed a little more, but then I started feeling sick.

"Are you ok Lena? You look pale."

"Massive nerves I think. I'm getting ready to leave everything I have known since I left home. The stress of the last few weeks, I just don't know, my stomach is a mess. I think I need to throw up..."

I ran back to the apartment and threw up. I felt better and went back to the truck.

"Feel better?"

"Yes, I guess. I can't begin to tell you how happy I will be when this is all over. How long did Patricia say this would go on?"

Cera didn't answer me, she just looked at me funny.

"What?"

"Nothing, lets hit the road."

We were off.

A couple of hours into the trip Cera asked if I had called my parents to let them know I was coming back to Colorado.

"Oh hell no! Why would I do that? First I would hear no end of the hells that involved Geoff. Second, they would immediately lecture me on my piss poor decisions. Finally, they would hang up on me but not before telling me not to call asking for money ever again, even though I wouldn't have asked for shit. No, I am not calling them."

"You don't think they have gotten over it yet?"

"Really Cera? My parents? Mr. and Mrs. Perfect? No. I made my bed, I can lie in it, that is exactly what they would say. I won't be calling them."

Jill Edick

"I know you don't want to, but what about money. You don't have very much. I'm not worried about rent, but what about groceries and school stuff for the girls and utilities and stuff? Until you find a job you're going to need some money. You really don't think they would help you a little?"

"No Cera, I don't. I'll figure something out. Thanks for worrying about me. But I really can't call them."

"Well, what about Kendall? I bet he would give you some money especially now that he isn't paying for the security detail. Thank goodness Patricia finally got rid of the media. What a cluster fuck! Honestly"

"Oh, I can't call him begging for money, he has done way too much for me already."

"Lena! He loves you! Let him help you! You're going to have to call him sooner or later anyway, and you need the help. You're really going to need help once you pull your head out! Call him!"

"What are you talking about Cera?"

"Nothing. I'm hungry, let's get some lunch!"

We stopped and ate, then drove on, then stopped for dinner then drove on. Then stopped for the night. Got up the next morning and BAM! Sick again! What the hell was wrong with me! I decided to blame it on Iowa and let it go. Cera just smiled at me but didn't say anything.

We drove on and on and finally late that night we pulled into Cera's parking space. Well spaces actually. We were absolutely exhausted and I fell immediately to sleep with plans of sleeping until noon.

Well, the best laid plans. I awoke early as usual but not because I woke early, but because I was sick again. I started to panic. I hadn't been sick like this since..... OH CRAP!

No, No, NONONONONONOoooooooo!

I opened the door to the bathroom and Cera was standing there. "Figure it out yet sweetie?"

"FUCK! Cera! Fuck!"

"Yes, that is what caused your little surprise I believe. Want to confirm it?" She handed me a pregnancy test and walked away.

She yelled from across the house, "Call him!"

I panicked. I couldn't be. I was 35 years old for crying out loud. I had three kids already. I had a mountain of debts, no house, no car to hold the brood I had, no job, no money, how the hell did this happen???

I started the pregnancy test and while I sat there waiting for the results I thought back to 'the night'. Didn't we use protection, I brought condoms...then I remembered. That first time on the sofa, it was intense and happened so quickly, we never stopped for the condom. I looked at the stick and there it was, the pink line for 'congratulations' was there.

There was a knock at the bathroom door, "Lena?"

I opened the door and held out the stick for Cera to see.

"Well congratulations honey. You ready to call Kendall yet?"

"I can't call him. And tell him this?? Are you kidding? It's not like I can move across the world and be with him, I have three other kids. He's a business man in another country, it's not like he can just walk away from that. FUCK!!!!"

"Lena, it's his baby too. He has a right to know. He has a right to make his own decision here."

I knew she was right, but I just couldn't wrap my head around this. I was freaking out.

"Lena, you need to get it together. Jena is bringing the girls down in about an hour. You need to pull yourself together so you can see them and start your new life here. You're not doing yourself or the baby any good falling apart. I don't mean to be mean, but you need to snap out of it now. There is no time for self-pity here."

"I know, I know. I just, just, pregnant. Shit. OK, OK, I can do this. I can. Let's do this."

I stood up and wiped my eyes. "Thank you Cera, you are the best."

"Well name this one after me then. Come on, I want to take you to your new place neighbor!"

"Neighbor?"

"Yup, you will be sharing walls with me. Lucky you! You won't be able to pull anything over on your landlord. Buwahahahahahaha!"

She cracked me up! That was exactly what I needed.

Chapter 29

We went next door.

"I had the place cleaned when my friends moved out. But it could certainly use a coat of paint and the carpets are out of here! I hate carpet. I will get this shit replaced asap. But it does have three bedrooms and two bathrooms at least, so you should be comfortable. I had the electricity and gas turned on in my name for now. You can get that switched over for next month."

"This is great Cera. I can't thank you enough."

"Well you haven't signed the lease yet. Wait 'til you see how much your rent is." She was laughing then.

We started moving in some of the things from the truck. We were about half way through when the girls arrived.

It was so awesome to see them. We all hugged and I bawled, then we went through the house and of course the girls all tried to claim the master bedroom. I told them they could all three share it and I would get the other two rooms, but that didn't work for them either, finally we had the rooms sorted out. The girls had brought sleeping bags with them to sleep in for the time being. Jena's husband backed their truck up and started to unload a sofa and chair into the living room and a small table and chairs into the kitchen.

"Where did this come from?"

"Cera has been storing a bunch of stuff in our garage for a while until she decided what she was going to do with her life. She asked us to bring it down so you would at least have a few things to get you started."

"I have a double bed at my place too that no one ever uses. We can bring that over later for you Lena. We'll figure out something for the girls later. You can use my washer and dryer as well for now. Maybe we can find a set for you at a refurbished appliance store that doesn't cost a fortune. Maybe I'll even buy a set, that should be a bonus for future renters if there is already a set here."

"Your all are so wonderful. We appreciate all you have done. I can't say thank you enough Jena for taking care of the girls for me for two months! I so owe you! And Cera, wow, just wow. Thank you! I updated my resume before we left and my former manager sent me a beautiful reference letter, so I should be able to find a job soon and I can start repaying you all!"

"You owe us nothing. This is what friends do! And wait, your boss wrote you a reference letter? I thought they wouldn't let you come back."

"That's what she said when I called, but she e-mailed the letter and said that they just couldn't have me back because of potential backlash in the area, I understand that. But that didn't change that she said I was a great employee and wanted to help me any way she could. So I at least have a good reference, my new name and a few good skills."

"Great attitude Lena! You're going to find something quickly."

We spent the rest of the week painting and Cera had floor people come in and rip out carpet and new floors went in. Jena brought down her air mattresses for the girls to use since there was no carpet any more.

I started sending out resumes like crazy and had several calls on Monday. By the end of the week I had a transcription job at a nearby office. I was expected to come in to the office for at least ten hours a week, but the rest of my job I could do from home which was great. I took what little money I had left and bought a desk to put in my room for work. My first paycheck I got the utilities put in my name and gave Cera a little money for rent. Things were improving. My next check I promised the girls we would look for some furniture.

I finally mustered up the courage to go see Cera's doctor. After an ultrasound, there was no doubt, I was pregnant. From the looks and sounds everything was great, the baby was exactly the size it should be and appeared to be developing good. Because of my age though, she wanted to do another ultrasound in a couple months and possibly more tests depending on how that ultrasound came back.

I had not been brave enough to tell Kendall. I had actually stopped calling him. I wasn't real sure what I expected from him or what I wanted. So I just started avoiding him. I had stayed up and looked at the stars a few times, but not like I should and I felt bad. I wondered if he was still looking at them and thinking of me or if he was getting over me.

I cried myself to sleep most nights. Cera told me off most days for not calling Kendall and not telling the girls about the baby. I guess I was in a state of disbelief, maybe denial. I wasn't sure. I just wasn't ready yet.

My dad called me one day and said he heard I was back in Colorado. He said he would love to come see me, but it would be best if my mom did not know about it. I declined and told him that I wasn't going to play the secret game. I wouldn't lie, I had had enough of lies to last me the rest of my lifetime. If he couldn't stand up to her and she couldn't not be a bitch, then it would be best for him to stay away. My daughters didn't need to lose another man in their lives before they even really knew him.

Chapter 30

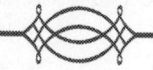

Across the World:

It had been so long. Was she lost to him? He missed her. He thought of her daily.

His phone chimed then, he had a text. He jumped and ran to grab his phone, maybe this time it would be her.

It wasn't her, but someone who knew he needed to hear from them. The text was short, but he jumped, not needing to be told twice. It said: GET HERE!

The days turned into weeks, summer into fall. The girls started their new schools and I was over the morning sickness but my clothes were all getting tight and uncomfortable. I had found a small car to buy. It was old and not beautiful, but it had enough room for all of us. Cera financed me. I was truly blessed to have her. Well until she started nagging me about Kendall.

I know she was right, I just didn't know how to even proceed now, so much time had passed. I certainly had a knack for screwing things up where he was concerned. I was so sad and I missed him so much. I was totally confused what to do.

Cera said I was wrong to not call him and wrong to be denying him the opportunity to see his child growing and developing. I knew she was right and I was sick about it.

After I dropped the girls at home after school one beautiful fall afternoon I went to a nearby park and just sat. I sat on a bench and just stared. I wanted Kendall. I loved Kendall. I didn't know how to fix the mess I was sure I had made.

Truly

As I sat alone on the cool park bench, I couldn't' t help but wonder what is happening on the other side of the world. As our night sky darkened and the stars started to make their appearance, I wondered as I looked up, can the people across the world see the same stars as I? And I'm thinking where is my heart right now? Is he thinking of me? What happened to my life? Will I ever feel whole again?

From behind me I heard "That one is Perseus, the hero. Did you know that on the other side of the world people see the same stars?"

I jumped about a mile. I turned to look and there was Kendall. As usual his appearance rendered me speechless.

I managed to squeak, "Kendall".

"My love?"

The tears started falling and he took me in his arms.

"Lena, please tell me you still love me! I have been dying inside not hearing from you. I have never in my life felt this way before and I know I will never feel it again. I love you I love you I love you! Please say you feel the same."

"Kendall, I do."

He pulled me close. Then he went still. He looked down at me then pushed me back a little and put his hand on my stomach.

"LENA?"

"I'm pregnant. You're going to be a father. I'm sorry I didn't tell you. I have been so confused. It's no excuse, I'm sorry, I just.."

He planted a kiss on me then. Then he picked me up and spun me around.

"Oh Lena! This is amazing! I'm here now! I will never leave you. Have you told your girls?"

Jill Edick

"No, only Cera knows."

"Well let's go tell them! I want to properly meet them and tell them how much I love you. Can we please?"

"I'm not sure how they will react, but, I guess they need to know. Kendall?"

"My love?"

"I'm scared."

"I'm here, and I know your scared. I'm a bit nervous myself. But I'm ready. I love you and together we will tackle the fear. Together."

Epilogue

Finally, across the country:

The headlines told the story: MURDERING SPOUSES FINALLY CAUGHT!

The story followed, but we paid no attention to it, they had been caught and we were safe.

The lawsuits were being sorted out, and life was returning to normal.

Now it was finally time to start putting it all behind us, and LIVE!

The sound of screaming louder than mine went through the room.

"IT'S A BOY!"

Kendall had tears rolling down his face as the doctor handed the baby to me. He was perfect. He looked just like his dad, he was a beautiful baby. Kendall came over and sat with us and started playing with the baby's fingers. The baby was crying and had a great set of lungs. I put my finger to his lips and he calmed.

"Well daddy, the agreement was you pick the boy name. What is your son's name?"

"I would like a name that my mother cannot shorten, like Kendall, so I think I would like to call him Keegan. That can't be shortened can it?"

"You know I don't mind names that can be shortened, however, I love it. Keegan is perfect! I love my men."

"I think this young man has some big sisters waiting to meet him. Are you ready Keegan? Your about to meet your big sisters!"

About the Author

Jill is completing a lifelong dream of writing and publishing a book with her first full length novel Truly.

She is in the process of writing a follow up to Truly and starting work on a new original novel as well.

Jill lives in Colorado with her family.